I0672938

Men's Chronicles: A Woman's Guide to Men Presents...

Lola, Lady of Sorrow:
The Side Chick
Volume 2

Sir Walter Jones

ISBN: 978-0-578-91302-5

Table of Contents

Introduction

Men sometimes say the darndest things to each other in private; it's the nature of the beast, I guess. One subject that obviously comes up is women and how attractive or sexy they are. Is this conversation only held amongst "worldly" men? Absolutely not, for I'm not around them a whole lot; I'm speaking of the clergy and businessmen.

Regardless of position or title, the average man has eyes, testosterone and "plumbing" that still works. That little boy in ALL men will rise up when you least expect it – whether in a courthouse, a business meeting, or Pastor's Study during worship. And who, pray tell, is often the subject of sexual matters? You've guessed it, "Lola." Why? Because she's easy like Sunday morning. Lola satisfies the lust of the eyes in men; she's easy to spot in a room and she's even easier to approach.

In Volume 1 of *The Four Women that Men Desire*, I explain how sex is Lola's superpower. She may have other talents, but she's mostly valued because of her sexual abilities and limitless desire to please her man. So, when men are in the cave together, they smile and giggle like little boys when speaking of Lola but cringe when talking about Phoebe, even though both these girls have similar traits.

Oh, sweet, sexy Lola, Girl A: The "Side Chick." What's in a name? That's not important; boys just wanna play in the sandbox and Lola doesn't need a formal invitation.

The story you are about to read is based on true life events. The names have been changed to protect the innocent.

Chapter One:
Memoirs of a Freak

"How come y'all don't have better magazines in this place?" Lola shouted out from beneath the hair dryer in her favorite salon. "This stuff is Old! I need to see some Vogue, or some Glamour up in here!" she laughed aloud, to anybody who would hear her.

It was Friday morning, and she was getting ready for date night. As she sat in the chair, she went over in her mind the things that she needed to do for the evening. Lola was never sure just when Calvin would appear at her door, but she always wanted to be ready for their late-night escapades. She had given him a key to her apartment, and he mostly used it during the wee hours of the night after the kids were asleep. Lola's "me time" ritual usually went a little something like this: a quick trip to the liquor store, stopping by Kroger's to stock up on "his" favorite snacks and making sure she was looking good! All in that order.

"Girl, that's cute!" she could overhear Tiffany saying to the lady seated in her styling chair. "Next time bring more bundles so I can try out that new style we talked about!"

Lola looked the woman over from head to toe and thought, *all the hair in the world is not going to change bad taste and style choices. And that cheap knock-off perfume she was wearing just reeked of desperation. This woman must not have a mirror or a friend!*

Lola laughed to herself as she continued to flip through the magazine trying to determine where the fragrance tab that was smelling so good was located. Once she found it, she carefully tore it out and proceeded to rub it on the inner side of her wrists.

"This is nice. I wonder who makes it" she whispered, inhaling the paper fragrance deeply.

Bundles was a small hole-in-the-wall hair salon on the East side of town, and it was Lola's go-to place for all things beauty. She loved the "ghetto-ness" of it all. From the random drunks hanging outside begging for spare change to the guys selling DVDs out of the trunks of their cars; Lola loved it. It reminded her of times past when she would lay listening to what she called "ghetto sounds" rocking her young son to sleep. The laughter in the shop, listening to the latest gossip, flirting with the walk-ins were the things that she lived for.

The best thing about the shop was the "No Kids" rule. It was strictly a grown-folks place to talk about grown-folks' stuff. The laid-back, lively atmosphere made her forget her troubles and feel as if she was out for a girls' only night. The strong scent of chemical relaxers and the fans blowing to alleviate the caustic smoke from Silk Presses and Keratin Treatments were all a part of the shop's charm.

Every two weeks, this was her Friday ritual. She had a standing appointment with her friend Tiffany to come into the salon at her leisure and get her hair done. From Lola's way of thinking this expense was as necessary to her budget as buying groceries. There was no doing without it, and she always made a way to make it happen. Sometimes one of her many "friends" would pay to have her hair done for her;

otherwise, she would cut back on something somewhere in the budget. Whether it was a payment arrangement with the Electric Company, Water Company, or being late with the rent; Lola was going to "do Lola" and make it happen.

One time she wanted extra money to party, so she faked a trip to the emergency room at the local hospital. With one phone call to her son's father for "supposed" medicine, Lola was able to secure enough funds for a new outfit as well as drinks that night.

"One of these days Willie is going to catch on to your foolishness" her friend Rita, would tell her.

"What Willie doesn't know, won't hurt him! Furthermore, he is not my man; he is only my baby's father!" Lola would quickly respond.

The mood in the salon that day was light and carefree. Jokes filled the small salon and Lola had come from beneath the dryer and was finally in Tiffany's chair. As Tiffany began the arduous process of French braiding her hair back for her sew-in, Lola caught a glimpse of Artie in the mirror and called him over for a food run. It had become customary in the shop to send a runner out for fast food and today was no different.

"Don't forget to bring me back some honey with my order!" Lola called out to Artie extending a ten-dollar bill to him from under her smock. "Make sure they put plenty of honey in the bag, too. Oh, and a Diet Coke too" she shouted out after him.

The four-hour hair marathon that she had begun earlier that morning was nothing new for Lola. Her days in the salon played out like a Soap Opera. She would chit-chat with other patrons, order food during the "food runs" and she always made sure her phone was in hand and powered-up with her standby charger. Lola liked sitting at Tiffany's workstation because it was situated upfront in the shop looking out into the street where she had a bird's eye view of all things.

She flirted with the regular delivery men, and on this day as she settled in her chair her eyes caught a glimpse of the finest thing she had seen in the form of a man in a long time. She sat up straight in the chair and crossed her long legs, slowly extending them so that the delivery guy might get a glimpse at the upper part of her thigh. She quickly lifted one of her eyebrows and ran her tongue across her lips to let him know that she was indeed watching him. The young man didn't stand a chance...

All of her adult life Lola had been told by men that she was beautiful. She had a nice figure, which included a cute little butt, a slim waist, and long legs. She was tall with lean, muscular arms and could eat anything that she wanted to eat without worrying about getting fat. Her thighs were thick from her high school days on the track team, and her breasts was perfectly symmetrical and shapely, and they sat erect and firm upon her chest. The fact that she suffered from Cystic Acne with the evidence of scars didn't seem to bother the men. She overcompensated for her facial issues with less clothing, skimpier outfits, tighter pants, and revealing blouses.

"Use what the good Lord gave you" was the mantra she had learned from her mother. Whenever she had a bad day at school or was being made fun of, Lola always found solace in the constant hammering of her mother's voice in the back of her head.

In response to any insecurities which she may have felt, Lola spent hours poring over "how to" YouTube videos on covering acne scars with the proper concealers and foundations. After all, when strutting down the street, it was her that the men noticed. There was something about the effortless way in which she strolled down the street that caused traffic to stop and men to whistle.

Lola had learned to keep her insecurities hidden, her feelings hidden, and her pain hidden. It was something that she was masterful at. No one would ever hurt her because she had learned to wear everything and everybody as a loose garment. She dodged before she was to be hit, and she left those in her life before they could leave her. If Lola wanted to be with a man or a woman, she was the one doing the choosing; if she loved a man or a woman, she was the one doing the loving. It was all on her terms.

But the one thing that Lola could not control was her sexuality. She had no real insight into her impulses. Whether it was another trip to the clinic for an antibiotic after a careless weekend of unprotected sex or the promises to 'be more careful' when undergoing yet another abortion; her sexual prowess was completely impulsive.

"Girl, I don't know what you did, but that was on point!" Calvin stated to Lola in a matter-of-fact tone as he whipped the covers away from her naked body and dragged them along with him into the bathroom. "I especially liked that thing that you did with your tongue...that was hot! Girl, you missed your calling..."

"Umm Hmm, I thought you'd like that!" Lola responded as she pulled herself up from the bed and into a standing position on the floor.

Coming up behind him, she gave him a little poke to his butt and continued behind him into the bathroom. Slowly, she squatted to her knees and pushed him up against the bathroom counter and took him in her mouth. The moans that erupted from his lips gave her a complete feeling of power and control.

"Thought I'd give you a little something extra to keep you coming back," she boasted after finishing her deed. With a side glance, Lola exited the room stopping only long enough to revel in the site of Calvin trying to recuperate from her pleasure.

Calvin was tall, dark, and handsome. He had noticed Lola in the local grocery store with one of his buddies and remembered asking his friend later that day about her "story."

"Naw, man, you can 'hit' that! We were just kicking it," his friend explained. "But I tell you what," he continued talking and grinned slyly, "You better eat your 'Wheaties' dude, 'cause baby girl is all of that!" he boasted and ended their brief exchange with a couple of fist pumps and a laugh.

Calvin wasted no time when they met months later securing Lola's telephone number. Two weeks had passed since their initial meeting, and when he finally got around to calling her, it was about 10:30pm.

"Hey girl, what are you doing?" was his greeting to her as she groggily answered the telephone.

Lola instantly recognized his deep, sultry voice and sat up quickly in the bed. She was no prude and knew intrinsically that this was her first "booty call" from her new admirer.

"Oh, nothing. Just waiting for you to decide to come and see me."

She giggled and settled back under her comforter to savor their conversation. And with that one call, their entanglement began. It had been eight months of late-night rendezvous, and every kind of sexual tryst imaginable between the two that lit a fire within Lola. Calvin had become her go-to guy for all things sexual. For Lola, it was the thrill of getting caught in compromising positions that seemed to excite her. When Calvin showed up to her job at the nursing home for a quickie, she was more than willing to oblige. The more risqué the sex, the better for Lola. She quickly led him off into the linen closet for an afternoon delight. The more danger involved, the more heightened her sense of pleasure.

One night, after a particularly exhilarating sexual romp, she turned to her lover in conversation and expectation and asked him to make plans to be with her at his home the following weekend. It was at that time that Calvin decided to tell her that he was married. Instead of the usual bouts of anger and feelings of betrayal, Lola quickly relied upon her wit and sharply turned the tables on him by asking him if he thought his wife would like to join them one night for a threesome.

"See, that's what I love about you Lo-Lo, you keep it simple," Calvin replied and continued to seek out his underwear from beneath the pile of covers.

To the outside world, Lola had the perfect life as a child. Born the youngest of three children, her oldest brother

Robert was away at college and her sister, Jewel, was a straight A student, a band member, and bit of a rebel. Lola admired her from afar, and their relationship was close. Jewel tried to be the caring big sister, but their age gap of 7 years had always been a barrier between the two girls.

As the youngest, Lola was spoiled by her father and tolerated by her mother. Nothing that the child ever did seemed to be up to her mother's standards or good enough for her. Her father was a long-distance truck driver, and her mom worked as a nurse. They lived in the best-looking house in the neighborhood; she wore the best and latest fashioned clothes, had every toy, doll, and game that she could ever want, yet she lived an isolated, and sad life within its confines.

Her Saturday mornings consisted of watching cartoon marathons, eating as many bowls of Captain Crunch cereal that she desired and doing her chores. Everything in their house had to be perfect, clean, and above reproach. Her mother always left a long list of things to do for the two girls, and they got them done. They put themselves to bed at night and saw themselves off to school the next morning. Clothes were laid out for the entire week under the guidelines of their mother and each day had its regimented meals and snacks. Sometimes, when her father was "off the road" and home for a few days, Lola could have company over to play as long as it did not disturb Cindy.

Her mother's third shift work schedule and sleep schedule seemed to be the focus of their entire lives. From the outside looking in, it all looked beautiful, ran like a fine-tuned clock, and was the envy of any untrained eye; however, Lola knew differently. As she sat alone in her beautiful room complete with matching bedspread, curtains, and rugs, she felt empty and alone. Lola's family secret and the foundation upon which she navigated through her life teetered upon the volatile fact that her mother was an alcoholic volcano!

Cindy was beautiful when she fixed herself up... Lola watched inquisitively as her mother propped her legs on the side of the bed and gently pulled the ultra-sheer jet-black stockings smoothly up her long legs. Cindy made sure she stopped ever so often to gaze at her reflection in the mirror and took her time slowly caressing her beautiful thighs making sure not to snag the delicate mesh. Often, Lola would sit on the bed and play with the nylon box from "Albert's Fine Hosiery" vowing that she too would one day wear something as beautiful.

"Where are you going tonight, Mama?" Lola asked her mother secretly hoping that her mom would take her along.

"What did I tell you about calling me, Mama?"

"I mean, Cindy" Lola immediately reiterated, trying not to offend.

"Why?... I told you not to be questioning me. I'm about to go out, and it's none of your business. Now, get off my bed and go play."

Lola got up defiantly and returned to her bedroom and slammed the door shut. A little later that evening she could hear her parents arguing in the kitchen. It was evident to Lola at that point that her father was not going "out" with her mother and that she would be spending the evening with her sister and father eating a T.V. dinner.

On Cindy's off days, she spent them drinking and

blasting old music throughout the house. At times, the drinking would go on for hours and experience had taught her girls to stay out of their mother's way. When silence would finally fall upon the house, Jewel and Lola knew that it was safe to exit their respective bedrooms and venture out into the living quarters to assess the damages. Most of the time they would carefully gather Cindy up from the floor, the kitchen table, or the basement and put her to bed always making sure not to cause too much of a fuss.

Cindy's half-naked body laying exposed upon her bed with her undergarment around her ankles was always a curious matter for Lola. She found herself staring in disbelief at the sheer sight of it all. She studied Cindy's nakedness with her bushy pubic area and couldn't help but to admire it. She wondered if she would ever be grown up like her mother. "Grown-up" in Lola's eyes meant that she would have large breasts, which seemed to get so much attention from the men in the neighborhood. "Grown-up" meant that she would possess the mannerisms that her mother displayed at the meat market when she was trying to get Mr. Palmer to throw an extra slice of ham into the wrapper after her mother slipped him a wink and a smile.

"See, child, you gotta use what the Lord gave you in order to get what you want!" her mother would say.

"Wanna see something funny?" Lola asked her young playmate one Saturday afternoon while playing with her in the family's den. Her father was asleep in his study and Lola was finally being allowed to have company over.

"Yeah, what?" Rita answered inquisitively.

"Come on," said Lola.

Rita followed her up the flight of meticulously vacuumed and carpeted stairs, through a small sitting area and towards Cindy's room. Thunderous sounds of snoring vibrated from behind the door as Lola giggled and cracked it open to expose her mother's half-naked and drunken body. Feelings of triumph and satisfaction came across her that day as she wickedly revealed her mother's state to her friend.

"She's so drunk! I could steal everything in her purse, and she'd never know," Lola pronounced to her friend, in a matter-of-fact tone.

And so, the two girls rummaged through Cindy's purse taking all the change and dollar bills that they could find and then fled from the room in a quiet heap of laughter!

"Now take that!" a vengeful Lola thought as she tightly pulled the door shut behind them. "Did you see all of that nasty hair between her legs?" Lola asked her friend.

"That was so nasty! Why didn't you just cover her up, why'd you show me all that? Ugh!" said Rita, while wrinkling up her noise in distaste.

The girls soon put all thoughts of Cindy behind them and went on with their play.

To Lola, exposing her mother behind her back was a way of blowing off steam. It was a way to make her mother pay for the secrets that she and Jewel were forced to keep. Usually, the young girl would have thrown the covers over her mother and closed the door after finding her in that state, but after the fight the two had last night, Lola was sick of Cindy!

She was sick of watching her mother sneak men through

the back door. She was sick of the late-night parties where she would watch her drunk mother on the laps of strange men. She was sick of it all! She thought that her mother was nasty, and she secretly wanted her to get caught. When Cindy threw that glass at Lola the night before because she hadn't taken her evening bath, Lola vowed to get even with her, and now the young child felt vindicated. However, those feelings of triumph quickly left when the streetlights came on outside and her friend gathered her belongings to go home. That is when the familiar feelings of emptiness and dread fell upon her.

"Thanks, girl," Lola said as she admired her finished hair in the mirror and stretched her arms over her head in an exasperating yawn. "This is nice," she complimented Tiffany.

I love it! Playing with her new head full of curls, Lola was imagining her upcoming evening. If Calvin was to be a no-show because of his "wife issues," she sure wanted to know in enough time to get a stand-by. In Lola's mind, there was nothing worse than spending a Friday night alone. She hated it. Even if her children were with her, she wanted and needed to be wrapped in the arms of a lover. There was no compromising about that! Somebody was going to love her that night.

As she paid for her "do" and was standing at the register stuffing the bills back into her purse, there he was; "Mr. Delivery Man" loitering shyly at the front entrance of the salon. As she reached for her sunglasses to ward off the rays of the sun, Lola took the extra time to fidget with her skirt seductively and tilted her head in his direction as she slowly pursed her lips to confront him.

"Are you stalking me?" she coyly asked stepping closer to him.

"Uh, no, just thought I would stop back around and see.."

But Lola wasn't waiting for long explanations or intentions; she jumped in before he could finish his sentence. "Like what you see?" she flirted with him slowly turning and flipping her hair in his direction.

"I love everything that I see," the young man replied boldly and paused to take an obvious head-to-toe scan of the young woman that stood before him.

"Well, here, take my number and call me tonight around midnight if you're free," Lola boldly stated without taking her eyes off his bulging biceps as well as the bulge forming in the seat of his pants.

"Wow, you're kind of bold, aren't you?" he asked.

"Well, when I see something that I'm interested in it doesn't take a whole lotta time for me to ..."

His laughter broke the couple's tension, and they continued with their flirty banter.

"My name is Lola, and you are?"

"Mike Welsh," he answered and extended his hand for a formal handshake.

"Well, Mike I'll wait to hear from you."

"Why midnight?" he asked as he deposited her number in the top pocket of his uniform shirt.

"Why not?" Lola snapped back.

And with that flippant response, she quickly sashayed away, making sure she displayed her full backside in motion! Nope, he didn't stand a chance!

Lola had to decide how she wanted to approach her "Mike situation". *This is going to take some finagling*, she thought as she turned out of the driveway of the beauty salon. Mike was fine, but she was in love with Calvin.

"Girl, don't you let that fine specimen of a man slip through your fingers!" Tiffany warned. "From what I hear around the shop he has no kids, he's not married, not seeing anybody special... and did I say he's not married? Every time he comes into the shop with a package, I have to pick up the panties off the floor," she laughed.

"Yeah, but Tiffany, a guy like that probably wants a little more than what I'm willing to give. You know the type. They want to take you home to Mama or take you to church. Those are two of the things that I have no interest in," Lola laughed. "I'm gonna holler at you later; the kid's school bus is here."

"Okay, Mrs. Welsh" Tiffany kidded her friend as she hung up the phone.

Chapter Two:
She Knows Her Place

The snow was coming down hard outside. Lola could see through her apartment window that the flakes were building up momentum and had the potential of becoming a full-blown snowstorm! *My, how the time flies*, she thought, as she collected the lunch she had prepared for herself the night before from the refrigerator. Willie was coming by later to take Little Willie with him for the weekend, and her other two kids would be spending the weekend with her father. It had been a while since the kids had spent some time with their grandfather. Lola felt excitement at the thought of having the house to herself for the weekend. Just thinking about the possibility of spending the evening alone with Calvin put a little "pep" in her morning routine.

Laying out a plan to be with Calvin was two-fold in Lola's mind. It usually involved him having to come up with an excuse to sneak out of the house and secondly, his coming over also depended upon his level of horniness. If Calvin was horny, he was going to find a way to get to her. If it was Lola who was feeling amorous, it meant that she either had to wait for his call or pull out her own "little black book." Experience had taught her not to upset the apple cart with sexy text messages or lusty memes. They were too dangerous and could jeopardize her fragile house of cards... a lesson she had learned a long time ago.

"Put that back cuz I'm not buying it!" Lola said to Ty

and Trina as she hurried them through the department store. She purposely took the route through the basement of Macy's to get to the center of the atrium and avoid both the crowds and the mall's other distracting points.

"I don't wanna hear you guys talking about going into the arcade, stopping at the skating rink, or the food court," she warned the two during their drive to the mall. "We are going in there for one thing and one thing only and that's to see Santa Claus. We're going to take these pictures for your Granny and then we are hitting the door! Everything else we can do another day!" Lola firmly explained.

"Ooh, Ma!" Tyson piped in, "can we stop and get a Cinnabon?"

"No!" Lola reiterated, "what did I just say?"
"Awe, man!" the 7-year-old fumed and went back to his hand-held game unimpressed with the day's itinerary.

"Go on up there, Ty we're next! Don't be so scary Trina," Lola instructed the two.

As each child stepped up onto the ramp and into Santa's lap Lola pulled out her cell phone and took a few quick pictures. Their visit seemed to be taking forever, and Lola began waving her arms at them hoping to bring an end to this annoying ritual. The children finally caught the hint and reluctantly made their way back to their mother who was clearly "not feeling it" and ready to go.

Whew, she thought, as she pulled the seat belts across each child's lap. *I will be so glad when this season is over.*

The holidays for Lola were challenging to say the least.

They were a constant reminder of what she didn't have. The shopping trips to the mall, stuffing stockings, the tree, the ornaments, buying gifts, the lists, the wants…these were all the things built into Christmas that Lola could do without. To make matters worse was the constant fighting with her kid's fathers. Trying to figure out who was going where with whom and at whose expense gave her a headache and was an ordeal that she dreaded! The only thing that she wanted from these men was their paychecks and for them to commit to scheduled time with their kids. Anything else was of no interest to Lola.

Not having Calvin to share the holidays with openly was irritating to Lola and something that she could only admit to Tiffany. Fantasies of them enjoying a family Christmas together had now been replaced with his promise of the "day after". The "day after" was to be Lola's Christmas. Calvin promised it to her, and she accepted it. She made it as substantial in her mind as the actual day of Christmas. Her plans were for her and the kids to spend the day with family, and the next day with Calvin. This was the "reality", which she had cleverly spun into a positive. A spin that she told herself she needed and deserved. It would be her sweet break from the norm. Lola always needed a break – mentally, financially, emotionally, and sexually! She always felt overworked, underpaid, and underappreciated.

When an extra shift or two became available at work, Lola jumped at the opportunity to take them. She was not afraid of putting in that extra time if it meant bringing home a bigger paycheck. With the lifestyle that she aspired to, there was never enough money. Lola had no heroes to swoop in and help. There was no one of means in her life to help her – not even Calvin.

He didn't play that role in her life, and she was careful not to mix their two worlds. Being with Calvin was about escape for Lola and her life without him in it was about domestication, which she frantically juggled.

"Mommy, are you coming with us to Granddaddy's?" Ty asked his mother as she buckled him up in the back seat of her car.

"No, Sweetie. Grandpa's been calling me all week to get you guys over there to see him. Today is for you guys, so enjoy it!" she firmly stated, letting him know that the subject was closed.

I have got to get a better caliber of friends, she thought during her ride to her dad's house that afternoon. As the kids sang their songs over and over in the back seat of the car, Lola tried not to let their monotony irritate her.

Calvin, Darnell, Mike, or any of the many men in her life could hardly be leaned on in her times of trouble; as a matter of fact, she spent a great deal of her disposable income on them. Lola loved to appear to have it all together. She never let on to them the fact that she was struggling. If Calvin came by, she made sure that her fridge was stocked with his favorite foods and beverages; if they stopped at a drive-thru for food, she made sure that she picked up the tab. Whatever it took to keep the flow of their relationship light and uncomplicated she did. After all, she was "easy breezy"... that was her motto.

Lola felt that her place was to be a point of release and relief for Calvin. She wanted to fill in the gaps of his life with the uncomplicated warmth of hers. It was to be a haven from all things domestic. As much as she wanted to be with him and enjoyed her time "sexing" him, Lola knew her place and how she fit into his life. She was careful not to nag or to be too demanding upon his time or his financial resources. Whatever was needed to make it a good night with Calvin, Lola painstakingly achieved it. Lola never let on that she regularly borrowed money from her kid's child support, or that she took out payday loans; it was part of the role that she played. When Calvin asked her what she was going to give him for Christmas the previous week, she simply responded, "What do you want?"

"What I really want is that new Apple Watch," he answered. "Now that would be nice."

"We'll see. Maybe if you're really good," she replied, lifting her eyebrow seductively at him as she stroked his chest.

That night Lola went online to price his request and the cheapest one that she was able to find was priced at four hundred dollars.

What the hell? She didn't know how in the world she was going to pull it off. Only Lola could answer the question as to why she wanted to spoiled Calvin so.

"Girl, that man got a wife!" was Tiffany's response when Lola shared with Tiffany her intentions of purchasing the watch for Calvin.

"I know, but he asked me, and I want to get it for him," Lola whined.

"What is he getting YOU? Just like I thought, nothing!" was Tiffany's retort.

Calvin's first hint at this watch came up earlier that month as they lay in bed. He joked with her about how cheap his wife was and planted the seed of 'the watch' right then and there! Lola, Calvin, and his wife Vicky had bumped into each other at the mall earlier that same day, and the three of them made "nice" under the pretense of catching up. The two pretenders kept their cool and never gave a hint of their dishonesty or deception. Although Lola had known Vicky since high school, the two girls weren't close friends, they were more like acquaintances. Their paths parted when Lola got pregnant with Little Willie and dropped out of school.

After the three "old friends" exchanged niceties, they parted ways. Lola stood off in the distance and watched them as they walked hand in hand towards the Apple counter laughing as if they were the perfect couple. She later wondered if that watch, which he asked her for, was the subject of the couple's attraction and conversation. Whatever the case, if his wife wasn't getting it for him, Lola surely would be the one to give it to him. That was the way that she operated, that's just the way that it was!

It was like a secret competition between the two women that only she knew existed. If Calvin were down, she would listen to his problems and try to be the one to make him smile; if he was excited about a new contract on his job, she listened intently, responded and celebrated with him. Lola thought he was the smartest, most handsome guy that she had ever met.

When Calvin complained to Lola about a particular sex act that his wife wouldn't engage in, Lola made it her business to be proficient at it. She wanted to be and do anything and everything for her lover. Nothing was taboo. She endured anal sex to the point that it had become their favorite position together and one in which she now

She Knows Her Place

enjoyed without the hint of discomfort or shame. The fact that his wife wouldn't allow these sexual practices in her marital bedroom made Lola feel as if she had more control and leverage over Calvin. Being with Lola was a crash course in control, rapture, and free sexual exploration.

"Dang, Girl!" Calvin said during one of their sexual marathons. "I can barely contain my erection with you I get so turned on! You're gonna have to slow it down!"

So, Lola slowed it down. Down to a series of long, hard, winding thrusts that caused him great pleasure and no pain. Like most things within their relationship, the sex was also one-sided, but Lola never complained. She secretly desired a session where she would climax first, and Calvin wished to please her. She wanted to feel his head between her thighs in submission to her desires as she was to his, but it never managed to happen.

When Lola threw her legs open and tried to steer his head between her legs, there was always resistance on his behalf. Lola, being the diplomat, acted as if it were of no importance to her at all. She merely finished herself off with the vibrator she kept in her nightstand by the side of her bed.

"Mind your granddaddy," Lola instructed her kids as she wiped the chocolate from Ty's face."

Lola's dad was getting older, and she was often concerned about his health. The divorce between her parents seemed to have taken a toll on him. What was once a broad, joyful smile had now been reduced to only traces of a grin. His once tall, lean, muscular form had now taken on a frailer, gait.

Leaving her father's house that day, Lola turned around to wave goodbye when her father lifted his voice in direct concern for his daughter. John saw so much of Lola's mother in her that at times it scared him. He loved her dearly and wanted nothing but the best for his youngest child, but he feared the path that her life had taken. Even though Lola thought that she lived a private life, there was always evidence of her "ways" which were visible to friends and family around her. At times, Lola's father was concerned about her contemptuous mannerisms and the irritation that she displayed toward her children.

Yes, John knew the signs quite well and did not know how to even broach the conversation with his daughter. The last thing that he wanted was for Lola to lash out in anger and alienate him as her mother had done so many times before.

"You know what Cindy? That's your daughter!" John sounded off to his wife. "You act as if she's a stray that you found in the back yard! If she got anything from you, it's her attitude! That's y'all's problem; you're too much alike for your own good!"

John hastily threw his clothing into his overnight bag and headed for the front door.

"That's right leave!" Cindy shouted in anger after him. "That girl is bull-headed and stubborn, and all you do is spoil her! In your eyes she can do no wrong! She might be your princess, but if she keeps disrespecting me,

she's gonna be a dead princess, I'll tell you that!
Walking around here like she's got all the answers…
I'm the queen of *this* castle and that girl has got
another thing coming if she thinks she's running
anything in this house!"

Cindy's shouts and screams could wake the dead, Lola
thought, as she listened quietly from the security of her
bedroom. The slam of the front door and the blasting
music now radiating from downstairs let Lola know
that her father had left the house. Lola locked her
bedroom door and pulled the blanket over her head.

It was seldom that Lola got into any kind of trouble at
school. However, when Kerry-Anne Mobley attacked
her in the hall over a rumor of Lola "making out" with
Kerry-Anne's boyfriend in the gym, Lola felt that she
had to defend herself. When the fight first broke out,
Lola found herself on the receiving end of the girl's
blows. She quickly decided that she had better defend
herself and the results were a full-blown fight in the
hallways of her Middle School.

"Pull her hair!" she heard Rita screaming from the
crowd. "Don't let that hoe scratch up your face!" her
friend instructed Lola, as the two brawling girls fell
back into the lockers that lined the hall.

"That's a lie!" Lola pronounced in rebellion to her
mother. "I wasn't kissing anybody! That girl is lying on
me, she was just mad because a boy in my 3rd-period
class said that he liked me, that's all; she was just
jealous!"

Lola continued to defend herself to her mother, but
Cindy was not swayed. It seemed to Lola that her
mother had come to her conclusions and whatever Lola

said went in one of Cindy's ears and out of the other. She could tell by the expression on Cindy's face that she was livid.

"Take your behind upstairs! and take those school clothes off!" she yelled at Lola. "If I've told you once, I've told you a million times that you go to school to learn and not to screw around!"

Cindy hurled all manner of insults at her young daughter as she pushed, slapped, and followed behind her up the steps.

"...And here you are coming home from school expelled after the principal called me and told me that you were fighting in the hallways like a thug! You think that you're a thug now?"

Cindy poked and pushed at Lola, and it was all that Lola could do to keep her balance. With each slap to the back of Lola's head, and with each kick that she felt to the back of her legs, Lola kept walking and fighting back her tears.

Her mother was relentless, "Huh? Is that what you think? I'll show you a thug! If you want to fight somebody with your bad self, fight me!" she demanded, pressing her daughter up against the railing and shouting into Lola's face.

"I'm so sick of you, Lola!" Cindy said in an unwavering resolve to her daughter as she watched Lola finally give in to her tears and collapse into a weeping ball at the top of the stairs. "Now, get on up those steps before I put my foot in your behind..."

Lola tried to bring her sobs under control. She watched

her mother from her porch between the balcony's posts as Cindy walked back into the kitchen and opened the liquor cabinet. It was the only thing that mattered to Cindy. It was the way she ended every confrontation in the house; by reaching into the liquor cabinet and pouring herself a glass of brown liquor. Lola hated Cindy.

Yeah, that's right, Lola thought, as she wiped her face. *Everything is always my fault and your excuse to get drunk!* She slammed her bedroom door fiercely and turned on her radio to drown out the thought of Cindy.

"I bet she won't be messing with you no more!" Rita re-assured Lola as the girls whispered on the telephone that evening. "You beat her butt! Girl, I didn't know you could fight like that. You were an animal!"

"Shoot, she was getting on my nerves trying to pull my hair out! I'm not trying to be bald-headed like her!" Lola responded.

Lola laughed through the pain of the day's events with her best friend only to be slapped back into reality by her throbbing headache.

"Daddy, when are you coming back home?" Lola asked her father after she answered his phone call.

John made it his business to call Lola a few times a week when he was away. With Jewel and Robert out of the house, he was concerned about the amount of time that she spent alone. John also knew of the cantankerous relationship that Lola had with Cindy.

"I'll be home after I make this run up the interstate," he answered. "I should be home by Thursday. You just remember to mind your mother and try to stay clear of trouble, will you do that for me, Lo?" John asked his baby girl.

"Yeah, Daddy, but I don't even be doing nothing and Cindy…"

John interrupted his daughter's sentence before she could finish. " I know, I know, Lo-Lo, but you know how your mother is."

Lola quickly changed the conversation to something other than Cindy and told her daddy that she loved him and hung up the phone. Her head was killing her.

The house was quiet that night when Lola awakened from her nap. Her head was banging with the worst headache that she had ever experienced. She knew that she was probably home alone because Cindy had gone to work. Lola got up to check all the doors and to turn on the alarm system. It was natural for Lola to spend her nights alone. With Cindy away working third shift she could do as she pleased and enjoyed being home alone; it made her feel like the woman of the house. Sometimes Lola would imitate her mother by pouring herself a drink while dancing to Cindy's old records in her pajamas. But tonight, all that Lola could think about was getting something for her headache.

The soft moans and whispers coming from her parent's bedroom startled Lola, and she crept closer to see what was going on. As she made her way to the half-opened door, she could hear her mother's voice and the moans of an anonymous male who was not her father. Through the crack in the door, Lola watched her mother and her lover engaged in the most obscene and graphic sexual acts that she could imagine. Shocked and speechless, the girl didn't know whether to scream or to watch, so she did both. The images of Cindy with her long legs spread open masturbating herself in front of this man caused Lola to gasp. It was more than she wanted to see so, Lola burst open the door and began screaming at the couple.

"I'm telling my daddy on you!" she screamed at Cindy.

Showing no shame in her game, Cindy simply instructed Lola to "get the hell out of her room" and to "close the door."

"Cindy is a drunk and a whore, and while you were gone, I walked in on her and some man screwing in your bed, Daddy," Lola said calmly to her father the next night when he called to check on her.

She didn't care about the situation, the circumstances, or the repercussions; she wanted revenge, and she got it that day on the phone with her father. "Daddy, don't be a chump or a fool, Cindy does not love you."

John hung up the phone after his conversation with his youngest daughter stunned by the coldness and the casual way in which Lola had spoken to him. John realized that Lola was a force. She was indeed her mother's daughter, but John had his own plans for Cindy, which did not include the dictations of a child. He would handle Cindy in his way and in his timing.

Maybe it was the impending snowstorm that caused John such concern for his daughter, but whatever the case he used this opportunity to try and reason with his baby girl.

"I just don't understand how you could be as old as you are, and so unsettled Lo-Lo," John said as he fastened his robe to ward off the chill on the front porch. "Most girls your age are married and have a good job, and you are still grinding the streets looking for Mr. Good Bar. That don't make no sense..."

"Daddy I told you that's not my life, it's not my reality. I don't want a man trying to tell me where to go, or what to do. I'm living my own life by my own rules." She blew kisses back to her father, waved goodbye to the kids and proceeded to drive off.

Lola's reality was that she never really wanted to have children. She got pregnant before finishing high school, and because she thought that she was in love with Willie, she married him. She chose to keep their baby as an attempt at playing house, calling her own shots, and a reason to leave from under the roof of her mother.

Willie Sr. was a good enough guy; he worked on cars to support them, but Lola quickly grew tired of him and their meager life together. So, she took Little Willie and left. Her second child was from a later relationship, which ended in domestic abuse. Her youngest daughter, Trina, was the result of a secret affair that she had with her sister, Jewel's boyfriend, Nick. She always told her family that she did not know who the baby's father was and she and Nick continued to keep that secret so as not to destroy what remained of her relationship with her sister.

"What do you mean you're pregnant? You better stop playing with me girl!" Nick said to Lola, trying to keep his voice down.

All the way to the library that day Lola rehearsed what she would say to him. With two children already at home, the last thing that Lola wanted and needed was another baby. Little Willie had been accepted into 4-year-old kindergarten, and Ty just celebrated his second birthday.

"What in the world will I do with another child?" she asked herself repeatedly as she tried to come to grips with the news.

To be pregnant was terrible enough, but Nick was the baby's father. The revelation alone that Lola had slept with Nick was enough to sever her relationship with Jewel forever. But the fact that she was pregnant with his child would be a constant reminder of that treachery. The more that Lola thought about her predicament, the worse she felt. By the time the morning sickness set in, she knew she had to have a conversation with Nick.

She called him at work and asked him to meet her at the local library. The two of them had begun to sneak around behind her sister's back shortly after Lola caught Nick staring at her lying on their sofa. The look on Nick's face made Lola blush as he studied her body.

Jewel and Nick had been high school sweethearts and were inseparable. Every place that Jewel went, Nick followed. When Jewel went off to college, Nick followed. When Jewel landed a high-profile job at a pharmaceutical corporation, Nick also went to work for the same company. Lola had always admired their relationship and wanted to one day experience that kind of love.

When Nick's eyes followed the shape of Lola's body as she lay across her sister's sofa that day, the curiosity of what it would be like to be with him gained momentum.

At first, the two flirted innocently at holiday meals and outings, but then, the fantasies started for Lola. Remembering every detail of Jewel's description of him, added fuel to Lola's fire. She recalled her sister being so giddy when she referred to Nick's lovemaking skills.

"Girl you have not lived until you have had a guy make passionate love to you," her sister informed her. "When we make love, I swear he brings me to the point of no return!" Jewel continued. "I have never in my life met anybody that knows how to master my body like Nick! That man can take me from zero to 100 in 2.5 seconds!" she laughed.

Lola listened intently as Jewel described for her the first time that Nick brought her to orgasm. At the time, Lola intended to engage in a little "girl chat" with her sister; however, Lola could not control the urge to superimpose her image over Jewel's during the climatic details of the story. She found herself submerged beneath the steamy details of her sister's romance and she could hardly catch her breath.

"See. Lo, you need someone like Nick to settle you down," Jewel said to Lola.

The two girls chuckled at the thought of Lola settling down and continued their girl talk. Never in a million years did Lola ever think that she would breach that bond between them.

Was he really all that, she wondered, while she and Nick stood side-by-side washing dishes after a family function. Jewel had excused herself from the table and asked the two of them to hold down the fort until she returned.

She Knows Her Place

"I'll wash; you dry," Nick said to Lola as he got up from the table and stretched long and hard.

Lola studied his frame and allowed her eyes to settle on the thickness of his chest. She and Nick made idle chit-chat and flirted cautiously with one another as they performed clean up duty.

"I'll be down in a minute," Jewel called from the stairway. "I'm looking for my blue sweater!"

"Okay, take your time," Lola said fixing her eyes upon Nick.

As she went into the pantry to place the pots and pans in their proper place, Lola found herself face-to-face with Nick. She slowly crossed his body, lingering seductively and brushing her body across his. To her delight, she noticed the bulge in his pants and reached out to touch it. Nick grabbed her hand in protest, but suddenly changed his mind and firmly placed her hand on the front of his pants so that Lola could feel his erection. All pretenses flew out the window as she allowed her lust for all things sexual to take over. The exhilaration of being caught or exposed during their stolen moment of pleasure drove Lola into a frenzied, sexual fever.

After that encounter, it was effortless for Lola to get Nick alone. They had sex at his parent's home, in the back seat of his car at the drive-in movie theater, and even in the basement of the local library. Never did she stop to think of the effect that their tryst would have upon Jewel until now.

"Nick, I wish that I was kidding!" Lola replied standing in front of her sister's boyfriend trembling. When I noticed that I was late, I took a pregnancy test, and then

I went to see the doctor to confirm it, so don't talk stupid to me!" she said in a matter-of-fact tone. "I'm about 6 weeks pregnant."

"Well, it's not mine!" Nick shouted and threw his hands up in total denial.

"It *is* yours!" Lola raised her voice, oblivious to their surroundings.

The two sat huddled together at a small table in the corner of the library. It was Monday afternoon, and the building was practically empty. A young mother in a remote corner was reading to her young child, but other than that the two were alone.

Lola's head was spinning out of control with the reality of what she had done. Somehow, if there was no evidence of their affair, she felt there was no crime.

"How do you know?" Nick demanded.

"How do I know what?" Lola barked back angry and agitated.

"How do you know that it's mine?" Nick said slowly, making sure that the intent of his question was clear.

"Because I haven't been with anybody else since I left that fool, Myron!" Lola said sharply and began to cry.

How could we be so stupid, Lola thought to herself. She loved her sister; Jewel, and she knew that this would kill her. Jewel thought that Nick was the man of her dreams. When Lola would talk to her sister about her previous domestic violence issues, Jewel would always point to Nick as the example of the type of man that Lola should have.

"See, Nick would never do that," were Jewel's famous words.

In her eyes, Nick could do no wrong. At Jewel and Nick's engagement party, when Nick asked Lola for one last dance, she conveniently spilled her drink on his white formal dinner jacket and excused herself from the table.

The decision to keep baby Trina was a difficult one for Lola. It was more difficult than any of her prior decisions to abort.

"Lola please don't kill my baby... Lola, please," Nick begged.

"No one will ever have to know. I could never live with myself if we did that," Nick revealed to Lola.

"We?" Lola snapped, "what do 'we' have to do with my decision?" she asked Nick sarcastically.

"It was our sin, not the baby's," Nick argued as he got down on his knees and continued to plead his case for saving the life of their unborn child.

There was absolutely no way that Lola could wrap her head around the idea of keeping this baby.

"How in the world could we ever pull this type of thing off?" she screamed at Nick. "There is no way that I could bring another child into this world without the presence of a father! And where would you be?" she asked. "You would be somewhere 'living it up' with your new bride, and I'm left with another kid!" Desperate for the conversation to be over and for her to have her way, Lola cried harder as she tried to plant the seed of her 'reason' into Nick's thinking. "So, in your "happy-go-lucky life you get to sail off into the sunset?" she questioned him. "Is that what you're saying?"

"Look, Lo, how about adoption?" Nick said trying to reason with her.

"I am not bringing a child into this world only to have them living with those abandonment issues!" Lola scoffed.

Every place that Nick turned for reason, Lola met him with her counterpoints.

"I'm going to tell Jewel," he stated flatly, turning to look Lola in the eyes. Nick was steadfast in his decision and dared Lola with his eyes to "try" him.

Lola was shocked by his resolve and slowly began her challenge of him.

"You mean to tell me that you would jeopardize all that you guys have plus my relationship with my sister because of a belief?" she asked.

"It's more than a belief, Lo, it's about trying to turn our lives around and living in decency, girl!" he snapped. "I'll do it, Lo, I promise I will! I'm not going to let what we did in the dark result in the death of an innocent child! I have to live with myself, even if you don't!"

Nick's words slapped Lola in the face. Who the hell was he? Mr. Self-Righteous now? Prior to that, Lola only saw him as a stud. She attributed nothing else to him except a penis. Maybe this was the 'thing' that Jewel saw in Nick, but she had failed to see. Maybe Jewel in all of her 'Cinderella' madness had rubbed up against a frog with a tiny bit of 'princely' character.

She Knows Her Place

"Look, Lo, I'm not trying to come off all preachy, but you need a plan, and I have one that doesn't include killing an unborn baby."

"Nick!" Lola pleaded, "don't do this thing, you just don't understand... Jewel is not like me! Jewel is not like me! She feels things... she thinks that you are 'some kind of a god.' She thinks that people 'grow old together' and live 'happily ever after!' She is not like me!" Lol cried.

"Shh," Nick said, comforting Lola as she fell in his arms. "Please Nick..."

"Lola you can do this; we can do this."

"But how?" she cried, "how?"

"Lo, we messed up, we messed up bad," Nick was now saying to Lola, "but we can turn this around, we can!" he said in a soft, caring voice. "Shh," he said again and rocked her in his arms. "Everything is going to be okay; I promise, I'll be the best god daddy that you've ever seen. We can do this, Lo, together we can do this."

For the first time in her adult life, Lola felt that she needed to surrender to a force greater than herself. And she made the life-altering decision to bring her daughter Katrina Renee into the world. Lola had decided to trust.

Lola rushed around the church, checking the flower arrangements, receiving guests and stopping from time to time to holler at her boys who were climbing on the back of their uncle, Robert. Bobby had flown in on the early flight just for his sister. It had been so long since the two had seen each other and Lola made sure that she presented herself in the best light for him. Robert was the one individual that Lola always wanted to impress. She knew that he was disappointed in her regarding her life choices and with the arrival of her new baby she was a little bit nervous about his judgment.

"Whatever he has to say," she thought to herself "I'll take it."

"My beautiful, tragic Lola," Bobby chuckled in Lola's ear as he held his baby sister tightly. The sight of Robert brought tears to Lola's eyes as her brother held her. Where had all the time gone, she thought as she held on to him not ever wanting to let go. All of Lola's fears melted away when he whispered into her ear that he loved her and always would.

"Please don't tell me that Cindy is coming!" Bobby said to Lola breaking up their overly emotional moment.

"I hope not, we can only take so much today," Lola laughed.

When Cindy did show up that day, both Robert and Lola steered clear of any conflict with her.

Bobby never returned home after medical school. He stayed in his small college town where he worked as a resident physician at the local hospital. His relationship with Cindy was just as troubled as Lola's. The embarrassment that his mother caused him throughout his life was something that Bobby had yet to forgive.

"Little Willie, stop running in this church!" Lola shouted after her son.

It was 2:30 and Lola walked into her sister's dressing area to bring Jewel her "something borrowed." Lola had chosen to loan her sister a gold bracelet given to Lola by their grandmother, Pearl. Lola could not help but smile as she saw how beautiful Jewel looked.

"Hey Lo, help me zip up my dress," her sister said as she turned her back to her sister and waited patiently.

Lola handed the baby over to Rita and slowly walked over to help her out.

"Oh, Jew-Jew," Lola exclaimed, "you look so beautiful!"

"I am so nervous, Lo," Jewel confided. "I keep feeling like somebody's going to pinch me and tell me that this is all a dream."

Lola looked into her sister's eyes and wanted to say a million things to soothe her, but all that she could do was to smile.

"I love Nick so much; we have been through so much," Jewel said.

Lola felt a pang in her chest as her sister confessed her love for Nick. The urge to confess all her transgressions against her sister emerged within Lola. It took everything within her to keep herself composed. She felt that Nick was not good enough for Jewel. She had gotten to know a darker version of Jewel's "Prince Charming" and he was a different person than Jewel described in her wistful talks. *Maybe it's just me*, she thought as she secured Jewel's bows and buttons flatly upon the bustle of her wedding gown. *Or maybe I just bring out the slut in men.*

Lola's encounters with Nick were nothing like the

warm, loving sessions that Jewel presented to her. The two of them tore at each other's clothing in utter lust just as she had experienced with all her other men. In her mind, she could close her eyes, and she would not have been able to tell Nick apart from any of her other lovers.

To Nick's credit, so far, he had kept his promise to Lola in taking care of Trina. Nick made sure that an overly generous check was in the mail to Lola every month and every weekend he or Jewel were available to spoil their godchild.

"What are you thinking about, Lo?" Jewel asked as she slipped up behind Lola while Lola watched Rita holding baby Trina.
"Oh, nothing," she responded and took her attention off the baby and back onto Jewel.

"It'll happen for you too, Lo," Jewel said and hugged her tight.

A tear fell gently upon the front of Lola's dress, but she didn't know why. "Weddings always make me cry," she laughed.

The wedding planner hurriedly entered the private dressing quarters and announced that it was time. Lola, Tiffany, and Rita all took their places in line while Jewel took their father's arm behind them. Lola convinced herself that she had done the right thing by keeping quiet. She could not for the life of her break her sister's tender heart. As the wedding party glided down the aisle, Lola couldn't help but laugh as Ty lost one of his shoes, and the flower girl cried all the way to the front of the church.

"Boy, kids will mess you up every time!" she said to herself.

The maternal feelings which Lola had for her children was that of restraint. She could never quite put her finger on why, but the result of her emotions led her to overindulge them. She made sure that they had the latest toys and gadgets that they wanted and paid close attention to how she dressed them overcompensating and obsessing over their appearance.

"Why do you have to buy that girl all the latest crap that she says she wants?" Jewel would always scold Lola.

"Because I can."

"Well, I'm sure they would rather have your time than all this junk that you're buying them." Jewel continued.

"Look, these are my kids and if I want to splurge on them, I will."

"But Lo-Lo I know you don't make enough money for you to be buying the latest Jordan's for a 7-year-old that doesn't even understand what a 'Jordan' is!"

"Look, these are my kids!" Lola reiterated.

"Whatever..." her sister said flippantly and continued looking through the half-priced bin for sale items. "Just don't call asking me for nothing... because I know it's coming. You have to start making better decisions and learn how to budget your money!"

"Girl, I don't have time to be visiting the local Goodwill, like you do to find decent clothes for my kids! We weren't raised like that, so I'm not going to raise my kids like that!" Lola stated emphatically hoping that this would silence her sister's constant interference in the way that she was raising her children.

Jewel rolled her eyes at her younger sister and shook her head as she continued with her shopping. She knew that there was no use in trying to reason with Lola about any of her parenting skills or the lack thereof.

Chapter Three:
"That's *Ms. Sugar Mama* to You!"

"Man…and I just got these nails done!" Lola fumed as she gingerly tried to turn the key and unlock her front door. She looked down at the chipped nail and tried to keep everything in perspective. Her nails had grown dry and brittle from the weather, and the reality of spending another twenty bucks on fixing her manicure was out of the question. But Lola was a bit of a perfectionist when it came to her looks, so she put a call through to Tiffany and asked her to fit her in for the repair.

"Take your coats and boots off in the hallway!" was her greeting to her kids after they arrived home from school. She hugged each one and promptly inquired about their homework. "If anybody's got homework, get to it. Your snacks are already on the table and wash those hands first. There's no telling what kind of germs y'all bringing home!"

Willie, Ty, and Trina had become accustomed to these after-school rituals and speeches from their mother. She had methodically gone over with them "ad nauseam" what she wanted them to do, and how she wanted it done. After years of hearing Lola bark out her orders to them, they now understood the routine and knew that their mom held little margin for error when it came to her rules. The children endured her endless speeches of "Pick up after yourselves, I'm not the maid," and her famous ending to every screaming fit, "I don't have time to keep picking up behind y'all!" and they tried to adhere, but because they were indeed children, and not Lola's robots, this repetitiveness continued.

Lola's children like most other children had no insight into her schedules and rigidity. Her need to keep a grip on the flow of her house was her conscious way of taking care of her needs and making herself available to Calvin. She always wanted to keep open a window of time in her day for a "quickie" with him or anyone else that she had the mind to be with. It was like watching in slow motion the orchestration of some great conductor. At times she seemed to be able to just "will" things into place; when that didn't work, she went on to plan "B." In Lola's mind, all this subterfuge, planning, and cajoling was at play for one reason, and that was for the sanctity of her "me time".

One of the surprising things about kids is their ability to smell a rat. This fact was true of Lola's kids. Their ability to discern character distanced them from Calvin. Their relationship with him was nonexistent. Calvin spent little to no time with them, and they politely went to their rooms when he showed up. This was not the case with Mike. The kids loved him! They spent time together laughing and playing video games; he interacted with them as much as possible. When Mike showed up to visit Lola, he usually came bearing their favorite fast foods, or pizza. Lola watched them one day as he rolled on the floor wrestling with Little Willie, while Ty and Trina ate pizza and watched their favorite movie. At times, the dynamics of their relationship was a point of contention for Lola, and she envied it because she coveted that position for Calvin.

Why couldn't this be Calvin, she thought as she spied on the four of them enjoying time together one Saturday night. In times past when Lola tried to include Calvin in a little family time, he stated that he didn't have "skills" when it came to children. That evening ended with the two of them sneaking off to the back seat of his car where Calvin was treated to the gift of fellatio to ease the tension that he said her kids caused him.

"Marry me, Lola," Mike stated suddenly and cuddled up behind her.

She lay in bed patiently watching The Steven Colbert Show waiting for him to come to bed after saying goodnight to her children. "Yeah, right," she said out of the side of her mouth and took another sip of her wine.

"I'm serious, Lo," Mike said and picked up the remote control and turned the volume down as he kept his eyes fixed upon her.

"Mike, stop!" Lola half-smiled and gave him a warning look. "Why do you always have to ruin it, babe?" She asked him jokingly and threw her pillow at his head.

Mike, sensing her sudden mood change, decided that tonight would be a good time to convey to Lola his true feelings for her. "Lo," he started to say but was interrupted by Lola's firm and gentle voice.

"Why would you want to ruin something as nice as this?" she asked him. Her voice was taking on a sexy smooth tone.

"Because I love you and I think we could be happy together, Girl!" he stated unapologetically. "And don't tell me that I don't mean anything to you."

Mike was a good-looking man with a steady job with UPS. He probably had insurance and dental too, but he was not Calvin.

"You've been seeing Mike for a while now, Lo," Tiffany said to her friend as the two women "power-walked" through the park.

"I know," Lola giggled, "he's a good guy," she said and continued to walk.
"I don't see what the problem is! You like him, the kids love him, why not take it to the next level?" Tiffany asked Lola.

"The next level?" Lola exclaimed, "I'm already spending more time with him than I should. He's catching feelings I know, and the kids are all googly eyed. It's not good, Tiff!"

"Why, Lo? I will never understand you. You run after the one person that you'll never have and toss away the one good thing that you do have... Girl, you better come to yourself!" she pointed out to Lola without missing a stride in her walk. "By the way, how was that restaurant that Mike took you to last night? I hear the lobsters they serve are always so fresh and delicious! See, girl, that's what I'm talking about! Calvin has never, and I repeat never, taken you out like that!" Tiffany remarked.

"We go out," Lola interrupted.

"Yeah, to Taco Bell! Not like the dinner you had last night, with Mike!"

Lola thought back on the previous night with its beautiful white linen tablecloths and fancy place settings. She loved the way Mike pulled the chair out for her and ordered her meal. The atmosphere in the restaurant was so calming and lovely. The music playing softly in the background felt romantic, and it made Lola feel like royalty. Mike had dressed up for the occasion as well. His tailored suit with matching shirt and tie made him look so handsome. Lola was the envy of every woman in the room. Everything about that night was the epitome of a woman's dream date. He was such a gentleman.

Lola wished that she could fall in love with Mike. She wished that she could abandon all thoughts of Calvin from her life and forge full steam ahead with a guy like Mike, but the domestication that Mike was looking for was the very thing that Lola wanted to run away from.

The idea of having to live the rest of her life without the benefit of hot, steamy sexual encounters in the back of the car or sneaking a quickie behind the building where she worked was not appealing to Lola. She wanted to be with someone like Calvin who excited her to no end. She needed the interruption of mischievousness to break up the monotony of her life. Between the kids, dishes, doctor's appointments and preparing dinners, Lola craved the escape of her sexual liaisons to free her.

"Shoot, messing around with Mike is not going to do anything for me but get me fat and pregnant," she laughed to Tiffany and preceded to take off into a full sprint.

Nope, tonight, Lola did not want to have this in-depth conversation with Mike. She was feeling amorous beyond words, and she knew exactly how to turn the tables. Their sexual chemistry together was good. When the two of them finally got together after having met at the hair salon, Lola was not impressed with the sex; it was nice and calming but a bit boring. It was on a softer, sweeter level; something that Lola wasn't used to. She was sure that it was satisfying for Mike, but for her, it didn't have the lusty depth that she craved. Lola wanted her sexual partners to be as aggressive, skillful, and in charge, as she was!

I do not have time to be teaching an old dog new tricks, she thought. Mike had not gotten Lola to the point of orgasm, and for her, that was the whole point of sex. She wanted the hair pulling, biting, and sodomy. Lola craved the dirty talk, the spanking and role-playing. The fact that she could bring a man to his knees was a part of her sexual portfolio in which she took pride. Lola wanted the reputation of being the "baddest chick on the block" and had no problem owning it. So, to steer the night in a different direction and to escape the subject of marriage Lola began to smother Mike with her kisses. She slowly undressed him and made love to him as furiously as she could. There was no sign of warmth shown that night only lust and her raw, animal passion. Domestication had left the building.

"I sure wish that I could meet this mystery man that's got your nose so wide open," Mike wistfully said as he kissed her goodnight and slowly exited her apartment door. As she stood in the drafty doorway clutching her robe to her chest, she let out a sigh of relief and headed back to her bedroom.

"Why couldn't Mike be Calvin?" Lola whispered. She would give anything to hear the words which Mike spoke to her come from Calvin.

Lola had stopped trying to explain herself to those within her inner circle who disapproved of her relationship with Calvin.

"Girl, you are not in a relationship!" her sister Jewel tried to warn her. "What you are in is a delusion, and when this bubble you've created for yourself bursts I don't wanna be anywhere near the fallout!"

"Is this a delusion?" Lola asked Jewel as she turned her computer screen toward her sister that displayed a hotel website with a confirmation code that was flashing. "All weekend just the two of us!" she gloated.

"Really," was Jewel's flat reply.

It wasn't a question which she posed to Lola as much as it was a response.

"Really!" Lola echoed and got up to do her little "victory" dance.

What she didn't divulge to Jewel was that the same morning Calvin and his wife Vicky had a horrible fight and Vicky had thrown his things out the door demanding that he leave, and never come back. When Calvin called Lola, he called her with instructions for her to find him a cheap motel to stay in for a few nights until he could get his wife to calm down and take him back. But Lola only saw what she wanted to see in this scenario. It was an opportunity for him to be with her. It was her chance to finally lie in his arms all night long and spin her web as the nurturing, "ride or die chick." A woman that would never leave him or be so foolish as to uproot him from his home.

What bothered Lola the most and the thing that she

would never admit to her sister was that after Calvin insisted on her finding him a hotel room, he never gave her his credit card number to pay for the reservation. He barked out the orders and left Lola to fill in the blanks. Calvin had plenty of money, but he was selfish. He never paused to consider that she may not have had the resources to complete this task. These were the things that Lola had allowed to get out of control with him in their relationship. After all, she had obligations that didn't include him.

The quest for Lola to be "all things" to Calvin clouded her vision. His cavalier attitude, broken promises, or even the times that he stood her up; they all went unchecked by Lola. She repressed his slights toward her and focused instead on what she called the positives; the way that he made her feel. The connection that she felt with him while making love was unexplainable. Being open and vulnerable to him, caused a surrendering of her body to him that cemented them together in her eyes.

Lola felt alive and powerful. Lying entangled in his arms, she barely knew where her body ended, and his body began. If he never went back home to Vicky, it would be her icing on her cake. But the couple's separation hardly lasted a week. It was a tough pill for Lola to swallow when Calvin called her the following week, from his bed, in his home, with his wife in the background.

It was Sunday night. Lola had prepared an early dinner for the kids, and as usual, she laid the kid's clothes out for school the following day and had their lunches packed and ready to go. Lola didn't know if it was the weather, a cold or just her achy bones that were making her feel a bit sluggish. She shrugged it all off and continued with her night hoping for a call from Calvin.

Lola had grudgingly spent the previous night with Mike because Calvin failed to show up. The vicious cycle that she sometimes found herself in when dealing with Calvin affected her mood. Just as she was giving up on being with him that night, she heard his key in her front door. Lola quickly slipped into the bathroom before he could see her to freshen up.

When Lola walked into her bedroom, she could see that Calvin was already unclothed and lay naked on the bed smiling at her. She wasted no time slipping into bed beside him. There were no long philosophical conversations or chit-chat about the weather between the two of them. It was not that type of party for Lola even though she wanted more from him. When Lola had something of importance on her mind or if something funny or interesting happened that day, she found herself wishing that she could share it with Calvin. However, he had long since told her that she talked "way too much" so, keeping it simple became her modus operandi.

"Hey, throw me a couple of bucks," Calvin called out to her as he pulled on his pants to leave. "I forgot my cash in my other pants," he quickly added looking at Lola with a sly smile and his hand out.

Lola grabbed her purse from the side of the nightstand and began searching through it in hopes of finding something to offer him. There in the back compartment of her wallet were two twenty-dollar bills. Without hesitation, she quickly slipped them out and handed them over to Calvin. The fact that she had laid that cash aside for Little Willie's field trip the next day never entered her mind.

"Thanks, Baby," he said, as he tucked away the cash, kissed her on the cheek and closed the door behind him.

"Ma, I need my permission slip signed, and Ms. Brown said anybody without their money is gonna have to stay at school in Mr. Davis's class today...Ma!"

"Dang!" Lola thought "How could I have forgotten about that?"

There was no explaining things to her son, so she made a quick dash into her bedroom to call Willie Sr.

"Girl, why you calling me so early in the morning about a field trip?" he asked.

"Look Willie, I don't have time for this. Your son needs some money and I need you to drop it off at his school before that bus leaves for the field trip. You should be glad that I let you be a part of his life! Especially when you do little else for him!"

Willie Sr. hung up the phone in anger but not before he sternly reminded Lola that his child support should have covered all their sons needs for that month. "I don't know what you're doing or what you have going on, Lo, but you had better get yourself together," Willie said in frustration and slammed down the receiver.

Lola held her breath during Willie's long list of accusations of her misappropriation of his funds and waited for the part of the conversation where he would give in to her demands because he always did. She waited patiently on the line tapping her foot and wishing that he would hurry up and get to the part where he said "yes" because her side was killing her. Grasping her side, Lola hung up the phone in relief that her catastrophe had been averted. She quickly yelled to

Little Willie that his father would be stopping by the school that morning to pay for his field trip.

Trying to get ready for work that day was seemingly impossible for Lola because of the pain in her side and the dull ache in her lower back. The pain traveled from her lower abdomen into her back and was beginning to scare her. Her chills and fever made her believe that she might be coming down with the flu. After nausea began and the vomiting started, she collapsed upon her bed and balled herself up in the fetal position. Lola knew that something was severely wrong. She lifted her eyes towards the clock which read 9 am. It took all her strength to locate her slippers, and she crawled to the coolness of the bathroom floor where she placed her hot face down against its cold, hard tile and she prayed.

"Oh my God," Lola groaned in agony trying to recall where she had placed her cell phone.

The cold compress to her forehead and occasional splashes of cold water helped very little, so she made her way back to her bed and called for help. As soon as Jewel picked up the phone, she could hear in her sister's voice that something was wrong.

"What did you eat last night?" Jewel asked as Lola tried to explain to her that she thought that she needed to get to the emergency room.

"I don't know, whatever it was it made me sick," she trailed off. "I need you to come" she pleaded with Jewel.

"Do you think that you need to call 911?" Jewel asked concerned about her little sister.

"No! Jew-Jew, come get me!" Lola whispered in a little

girl's voice that her sister hadn't heard in ages.

Her moans revealed a level of vulnerability that let Jewel know that Lola was really in trouble and needed her. She quickly grabbed her car keys and raced to Lola's apartment to see about her.

Lola could hear her sister trying to get to her, but she could not muster up enough strength to get to the door. Jewel pushed and pushed on the outside buzzer to Lola's apartment and when Lola didn't answer she frantically called 911 and waited for both the fire department and an ambulance to come.

The back-and-forth pace of the emergency room was intoxicating to Lola. She could hardly understand what was going on around her nor how she got there. Periodically, she would come to and see the worried face of her sister holding her hand and moving her lips. Jewel was trying her best to remain optimistic and upbeat. She tried to keep Lola calm by telling her corny jokes as they waited to hear from the doctor.

It had been a long day in the hospital's emergency room, and the waiting was excruciating for Jewel. She had never seen her sister so sick. Jewel stood beside her little sister and held her hand as Lola lapsed in and out of consciousness. The tubes, the intravenous lines, the beeping sounds of the machines monitoring Lola's vitals all made Jewel realize that she was in over her head. Jewel felt the need to call Willie Sr. as well as her father.

Willie could get the children from school, and she needed the comfort of her father. When Lola's hypoglycemia placed her into a coma, she was whisked away to the intensive care unit, and Jewel broke down and called Cindy.

Chapter Four:
When Emotions
are a Four-Letter Word

Lola's kidneys had been infected by what the doctors called Pyelonephritis. When her blood pressure dropped in the ER, it caused her to fall into a coma. Now, two days later, Lola yet remained unconscious. Jewel, Lola's Dad, her brother, Robert and Cindy sat beside her bed, night after night wondering if they would ever get her back. Jewel crawled into the bed with her little sister like she did when they were younger and when Lola was afraid.

Jewel thought that she looked so small lying there. She soothed her frail body with her soft caring, hands. She made sure not to disturb any of the tubes and wiring that were attached to Lola, and she continued telling her all the while that "they were all there for her." Jewel repeatedly encouraged her sister to open her eyes. When Lola did finally open her eyes, her dad cried, Robert thanked the Lord and Cindy left the room. There were no words between she and Lola, only the relief on Cindy's face knowing that with time, Lola would alright.

"What did you get on your MCAT exam?" Jan asked Cindy.

"I missed it by about 3 points!" she replied trying not to let her disappointment show. "That section on the

'Chemical and Physical Foundations of Biological Systems really messed with my head, but I will never give up!" Cindy proclaimed loudly mustering up her laughter to mask her disappointment.

For most of Cindy's life, all that she wanted was to become a doctor. She was an excellent student and finished first in her graduating class of 300. As the oldest child of Keri and Robert Barns, Cynthia, known to her family as "Cindy" had an unquenchable thirst for knowledge and was an ardent reader. When she was accepted at the age of 17 to a pre-med advising program at John's Hopkins, her whole high school celebrated with her.

The thought of attending this prestigious school and being put on the track to Medical school at John Hopkins was monumental in Cindy's world. She was wise beyond her years and focused. While away at school there was no time for "pledging" and late-night parties; there was only the desire to succeed. Cindy wanted to make her mother proud. Their relationship was close, and they were the best of friends.

There was nothing that she could not share with her mother. Whether it was a heartbreak over a boyfriend, the joys of window shopping, or planting tomatoes in their backyard, Cindy and her mom, Keri were inseparable. The cool thing about her mom, was that each child that Keri had felt the very same way. Each relationship was "easy-breezy" as she liked to say, and when talking to her mother each thought that they were the most important thing in the world.

"Phone call for Cindy," the housemother of her dorm screamed out into the hall.

Cindy lifted her head from her studies and curiously checked the clock on the wall.

Who in the world is calling me this late on a Tuesday night, she thought, as she put on her slippers.

The telephone booth was located at the very end of a long hall. Cindy rarely used it because she thought it was disgusting. It always seemed to be covered in some type of gook, was broken, in disrepair or someone was camped out on it in their private lounging chair. On that night, the walk to the booth seemed to take forever. As Cindy went to pick up the receiver from its now dangling position, she had a feeling of alarm. She listened to the voice on the other end but could not comprehend what the caller was saying. Her father's voice was soft and fragmented.

"You have to come home, Cindy; it's your mother."

During the car ride to the hospital, she tried to brace herself for the unknown. Upon entering the hospital room, Cindy headed towards her mother's bed. She immediately covered her mouth in shock at the sight of the frail, decrepit shell-of-a-woman beneath its covers. No preparation in the world could have prepared her for seeing her mother's body lying in that hospital bed.

Cindy tried to stay focused on the words that were coming out of the doctor's mouth. She tried to remember the last time she saw her mother.

"I was just home and saw Mama like three weeks ago,"… she repeated to anyone that could hear her.

"If you hope to attend medical school right after you graduate, you know you gotta complete those pre-med courses and take that MCAT by early May," Keri warned her daughter.

"I know, mama, I got everything covered," Cindy responded to her mother as she reached down and cuddled the cat in her arms.

It was the middle of her Junior year of college, and she had been inundated by the mounting tasks on her "to-do" list.

"I've got one more Lab to complete; then I'll be finished with all of my premedical coursework. I'm on it. I'm not gonna let you down," she smiled at her mother and gave her a wet kiss on her cheek. "That Biology 346 is my biggest worry!" she said in an attempt to bring her mother up to date.

"You'll do fine. Just settle yourself down and do like you always do," her mother encouraged.

That was the last conversation that Cindy had with her mother.

"What happened?" Cindy could hardly get the words out of her mouth.

"It's breast cancer, Baby," her father said slowly in a trance-like tone. "She didn't want you kids to know about it because she didn't want to worry you. By the time they diagnosed it she was already in stage four."

"Didn't want to worry us? What are you talking about?" Cindy demanded. "We deserved to know...I deserved to know!"

She laid her head on her mother's chest and listened to the raspiness of her labored breath.

"I'm here, Mama," Cindy said softly while kissing her mother's hand.

Keri and Cindy were known around their small town as the "Bobbsey Twins," and the older Cindy got, the more she enjoyed being in the company of her mother. There was something intriguing about her mother's Creole descent and the beauty of her thick, wavy hair. The many stories that Keri told her children of life on the Virgin Islands always kept them mesmerized. Keri taught her daughters the island dances and taught Cindy how to prepare her favorite dishes of fried plantains, dasheen, and cassava beans, but they never tasted as good as when her mother made them.

"This had to be going on for a long time. Why didn't you tell me, Daddy?" Cindy cried uncontrollably. "She can't even hear me! I can't even tell her that I love her. Why Daddy, why?"

Cindy was inconsolable. She felt that her complete support system had been ripped from beneath her. She stood stoic as she listened to the attending doctor rattle off her mother's prognosis.

"Stage four is the most advanced stage of breast cancer," he began. "Unfortunately, it has spread to your mom's lymph nodes, her bloodstream, her brain and most of her internal organs. It has metastasized," the doctor finished.

Shut up, Cindy thought to herself. "Everybody in here knows what metastasized means!" she fumed.

Fighting back her tears, Cindy looked around the small hospital room and into the faces of her sisters and brothers and tried to compose herself. What in the world would become of them?

"What does DNR mean?" John Jr. interrupted fighting back his tears.

"Come here Jon-Jon," Cindy said opening her arms to her little brother as she escorted him from her mother's bedside. There was no way that she was going to let her brother hear that their mother had chosen not to be resuscitated.

The anger, rage and utter sadness that consumed Cindy was insurmountable. Throughout the ride home, she teetered between so many emotions that it made her dizzy. Instead of her emotions finding a resting place in sadness, for some reason Cindy's emotions rested in anger. She would never forgive her parents for keeping such a life-altering secret from her. Her thoughts went back and forth to the nights that they laughed and talked as they poured over her college admission's brochures. Their late-night banter, her mother's home-made chocolate chip cookies when she was feeling sad, all these things were now gone from Cindy, and she felt cheated. Within two days Keri was dead.

Cindy walked back down the corridor of her dorm and slowly collected her belongings. No matter how her father begged her or told her that everything was going to be alright, Cindy could not bear to think of going back to school when her family needed her. She was the oldest of 5 children, and they were now her focus. The only mother that they had was gone, and her father was too busy working to care for them.

"My sweet Lo-Lo," Jewel began, fighting back her tears. "We've been waiting on you to wake up," she whispered to her sister wiping away her tears and giving over to the biggest sigh of relief that her body had experienced in years. "It's just like you Lo, to make a big scene to get all of us together." Jewel laughed and looked back over her shoulder to locate her mother, but her mother was nowhere to be seen.

Cindy had left the room and now stood on the other side of the door where she finally and silently broke down and cried. No matter how strained the relationship was between them, Lola was still her daughter and even if she never told her, Cindy loved Lola. She blew her nose on a Kleenex, threw the remains into the trash, and pulled out her car keys. It had been a long two days, and she needed a good, stiff drink!

Although Lola's doctors were able to catch the infection before it caused irreparable damage to her body, they warned her to stay under the care of her family physician. The cause of the infection was never pinpointed, but the attending physician gave her an array of scenarios. One of which included a build-up of bacteria in her urinary tract which seeped into her bladder during sex and subsequently invaded her kidneys. She was given a prescription of amoxicillin, instructed to stay hydrated, and avoid alcohol; she was reminded about the perils of having unprotected sex, and multiple sex partners. After she signed her discharge papers and gathered her things, Lola was helped to the car by her father; she paused in the fresh, damp air to inhale the sweetness of the breeze.

During the drive home from the hospital, Lola couldn't help but feel a little depressed. "I could have died in that hospital and Calvin would have never known," she lamented to herself and closed her eyes to shut back her tears.

As Lola lay in her bed alone recuperating, she hoped for a call from Calvin. Mike, Artie, Jake and even Willie had all made their rounds to see her, but Calvin was auspiciously missing. She wondered if he had even tried to call her during these last three weeks. Since her hospitalization, Lola had been keeping a low profile with the men in her life. Self-reflection was a hard thing for her. It took her to an uncomfortable place in her consciousness that she would rather steer clear of.

When Calvin did finally call Lola, it was with an air of flightiness and unconcern.
"Hey, Girl, what you got going on?"

Just the sound of his voice on the other end of the line ignited her smile. Calvin was a big charmer. The rich, layered, tone of his masculine voice always made Lola feel sexy. She could lie in bed with him for hours just listening to him talk. Whether it was him rambling on about his wife, his job or what have you, she could hear the rhythms and nuances of his voice and melt.

"I've been a little under the weather," she confessed, the weakness still apparent in her breathing. "As a matter of fact, I've actually been in the hospital for a while," she began saying but was interrupted by Calvin's interjection.

"Really?" he said, "Alright then, I'm gonna check on you later. Just thought I would see if we could get into a little something this afternoon, but if you aren't feeling it, I understand. I'll holler at you."

With the phone yet in her hand and the formation of words unspoken spilling from her brain, Calvin terminated the conversation. Lola tossed her cell phone across the bed and pulled the covers over her head. How could she be so stupid as to love Calvin? How could she allow herself to play second fiddle to his life, his wants, and his needs at the expense of her health? Everything that Tiffany and Jewel had ever warned her about him was true. "Never again!" she said and turned the volume on the TV remote control up.

"You have lost so much weight!" Tiffany exclaimed as Lola walked into the salon that Friday. "How are you feeling?" her friend asked as she ran up and greeted Lola at the front counter. "Just look at that mop on your head!" she continued, not letting Lola get a word in edgewise.

Lola slipped the silk scarf entirely off her unkempt head, and Tiffany gasped! "Oh, my Lord, it's worse than I thought! Sit down, take a load off; I've got you next in the bowl!" she laughed and escorted Lola into the seat at the sink.

It felt great to be pampered by her friend, and Lola loudly exhaled as Tiffany ran the warm, soothing water through her scalp. She thought that she had come full circle with her health scare and was back on top.

"Have you heard from what's his name recently?"

"Who?" Lola asked, pretending not to know that Tiffany was talking about Calvin.

"Who, my butt! You know exactly who I'm talking about; Mr. Smooth!" Tiffany taunted and turned up her nose not caring if Lola saw the distaste in her mannerisms.

"See, not today, Tiff!" Lola interjected. "We are not having this conversation today. I'm having a perfectly good day, and I don't need any bad news..."

"Oh, so he's bad news now, huh?" Tiffany joked.

"Well, you know what I'm talking about. I'm not thinking about Calvin. He is no longer on my radar; the Lord has healed me!" Lola exclaimed and pretended to throw her hands up as if she were attending a revival service at the local Pentecostal church.

"Well, alright then! It's about time you reset your dial from stupid to sane," Tiffany laughed and continued with the process of detangling her friend's severely matted hair.

Lola had made a promise to herself that she would put her home, her children and herself first. She felt as if things had gotten a little off balance throughout the last year of her life. Lola told herself daily that all she needed were order and discipline. She gave up drinking coffee and eating chocolate to alleviate her nervous disposition and was beginning to benefit from the effects of it. All in all, Lola was hitting her stride.

"How's my favorite girl doing this afternoon?" Calvin greeted as Lola picked up her ringing cell phone.

His call caught her off guard, and she sat down on one of the empty beds in a room that she was preparing for an incoming resident at the nursing home.

"Cat got your tongue?" he asked seductively. "Because if he does... let him know that tongue belongs to me," he said jokingly almost defying Lola not to laugh. "I need to see my girl tonight. I need to feel you, and only you in my arms. I've been missing you!" His deep, sexy voice monopolized the conversation, and Lola found herself being pulled back into his charms. "I've been going through some things," Calvin continued, "and I need somebody to talk to. Somebody that's not going to judge me. I need my Lola..." and with that simple conversation, Calvin found his way back into Lola's heart and her bed.

As far as him being MIA during her sickness, Lola chalked it all up to the prominent position that he held at his company and the demands which were being placed on him by his wife.

Their lovemaking was different that night when he slipped into her bed, Lola told herself. She thought that Calvin paid more attention to her body this time around. Instead of their regular primal-charged sex, for the first time, Lola felt that they were making love.

Somehow, Calvin's kisses were sweeter to her. When they kissed, it seemed to Lola that his mouth searched out for hers with such longing that she was sure it was love. She needed to believe that he had missed her while they were apart and that he loved her and could never live without his "Lo-Lo."

The connection she felt with him while making love was unfathomable and brought her to tears. The fact that she was so open and vulnerable to him scared Lola. The manipulative control that he asserted over her she would never confess. But Calvin knew it to be a fact. When they climaxed together, it was an all-inclusive and earth-shattering orgasm — an orgasm that told her that he was the only man that would ever be able to master her body. The only man who would ever be able to handle the passion of Lola.

Chapter Five:
The Vagina has No Face

Lola was feeling pretty good this morning as she stood partially clothed, dancing and singing in front of her bathroom Mirror. The bass on her DVD player was thick and loud and "bumped" just like she liked it. Lola primped and sashayed in rhythm to the beat of her favorite song. She paid special attention to the curves of her breasts. And crunching her stomach muscles to reveal its firm, washboard like appearance, Lola danced and sang...

"Make it smooth, take your time, make it groove, in, out, in make it last! kiss, kiss, kiss, kiss my ah, ah, ah! This is how it works; wrap your hands around my body. This is how it works; go due south"....

"Ma! Ma! open the door I gotta pee!" Ty screamed and continued to pound on the door to his mother's bathroom. "Ma!" he continued fiercely.

"Wait a minute boy!" Lola screamed back at Ty turning down the volume of her music and grabbing her robe. "I swear, I can't even go the bathroom in peace!" Lola complained. "What's the matter?" she screamed back at him.

"I gotta pee," the little boy pronounced again losing patience with his mother's questions.

"Why can't you use the other bathroom?"

"Cause Trina got her Barbie doll's head stuck in the toilet and it's overflowing... and I gotta go!" he pleaded to his mother as he pranced back and forth at the door holding himself.

"Judas Priest!" she sighed, opening the door, and surrendering her place of serenity over to her son. "Wait a minute," she said before he took over her throne. "Pass me the plunger!"

"I have got to do something about all of these bumps and dark spots on my face!" Lola told herself as she stood looking in the mirror after averting that morning's calamity of the flooded toilets.

She had tried to keep up her skin routine after her illness, but the acne on her face was a horrible site. Her skin had become dry and flaky with patches of dark spots and cysts erupting daily. She thumbed through her closet for the sexiest and most revealing outfit that she could find. Her trip to the beauty supply store had landed her with a thick face concealer designed to cover up the worst of facial nightmares, and she sat down at her makeup table to transform herself.

Lola's plans for the night were to be ready to go out for a long drive with Calvin. He called her earlier and told her he was stopping by to swoop her up for a bite to eat. Even though she knew they would probably just stop by the drive-through window of a fast-food restaurant, Lola wanted to look her absolute best.

"Where are you going all fixed up?" Calvin asked, as he opened her front door and pulled off his coat.

"Oh, I thought we could grab some burgers," Lola said.

"I don't want a burger," Calvin said, grabbing her firmly from behind and gently shoving her into the wall of the hallway while his hands caressed her butt.

"Wait a minute," Lola whispered.

"What?" Calvin asked biting her ear lobes and sucking her neck.

"The kids…" Lola began and ushered Calvin towards her bedroom and closed the door behind them. As Lola turned to face him, she stood against the door so that he might admire her outfit. She had chosen a deep plunging one-piece jumpsuit that contoured her body. The dip in the back showed off her round buttocks, and the suit clung to the shape of her thighs and left little to the imagination. To her surprise, Calvin had no interest in her outfit; he only had interest in his hand down his pants in self-stimulation. She looked curiously at him pounding his flesh in preparation for her because of the aggression he was demonstrating.

Before Lola could perform her rehearsed sexy little moves on him or turn around to show herself off, Calvin pulled her down to the bed and began pulling her clothes off. As he tore her panties off in a frenzy, she was trying to stay present in the moment. Usually, this kind of rough sex would have excited Lola, but it bothered her today because she had taken such care in the details of that night. Lola had gotten her hair done, her makeup was on point, and she had doused herself with her favorite perfume. The extra time that it took her to apply her acne concealer alone was worth a little foreplay, she thought as she suddenly felt the erectness of his body penetrating her.

"Hey…" she managed to say as Calvin pushed her head

down in her pillow and plowed through her body with the fierceness of a crazed man.

"Shh," he whispered, placing his index finger to her lips.

Determined not to be a victim, Lola played along. She abandoned any feelings of being overwhelmed, so she joined the party. If Calvin wanted her face down on the bed, she would submit to it; Lola rode out his storm. When he was tired of holding her down, she assumed the top position and "gave" as good as she got. Lola was not to be outdone. She was the master of her Vagina, not Calvin!

In her haste to get Calvin into her room that night and out of the sight of her kids, Lola failed to detect that he had brought his video camera along with him. When Calvin began to fumble around behind her, she quickly recognized the clicking sounds. His body never missed a stroke as he filmed them. Lola sensing his arousal at the fact that he was making yet another video of them for his collection began to play the role of his video vixen and gave him a full X-rated show of her prowess.

At lunch the next day during her break she laughed and whispered with a co-worker about her previous night's events. "Girl, I had that man coming and going at the same time," she giggled as Dana listened in amazement.

To most of the women who knew Lola around the nursing home, she was thought to be a bit of a slut. They watched her flirty ways and sexually boisterous dialogs with passing men, and they couldn't stand her. Lola was the type of woman that most of their mothers warned them to be aware of. Her uniform top was a size too small and always unbuttoned a little too far; her pants were form-fitting and revealed more than most women would want to show. The fact that she carried herself like she was God's gift to mankind was too much for them to bear.

Her early Monday morning recaps about where she went, what she did, and with whom she did it made her stories seem fabricated to them. But it never deterred Lola. She delighted in the fact that her body was perfectly formed, and men were attracted to her. She told herself that these women were jealous and that they envied her.

"She's gotta put out like that," she heard a voice laugh aloud from the break room one day.

"That's because her face looks like it's been beaten with a bag of nickels," another woman chimed in.

As Lola entered the break room for her cup of coffee, the women fell silent. This scene was something very familiar to Lola, but she held her head up high, grabbing her coffee and flaunting her 18-inch Brazilian, deep waves in their faces.

"If your man is not acting right, it's because he's not being taken care of at home, is how I see it," Lola commented in a matter-of-fact tone as she continued her conversation with Dana. "If your man is leaving you and going to another chick, it's because you aren't exciting to him anymore and he's lost interest! Now, trying to keep a man is one problem that I don't have." Lola said concluding her conversation.

She reapplied her lip gloss, said her goodbyes and left the break room.

"Hey, can you babysit again tonight?" she turned

around and asked Dana.

"Naw, I gotta visit my Nana at the hospital tonight. It's my night to sit with her."

"Oh, okay, I'll find something to do with them" she replied and waved goodbye to her friend.

The lies we tell, Lola thought as she pulled into the gas station on the corner of her house. She could not help but reflect on the conversation she had with Dana. If only Lola was as real as she pretended to be. She knew that Dana envied her, but Lola would never bring herself to tell the young girl of the many nights which she spent home alone waiting for Calvin to call. Nor could she admit to all the disappointment and feelings of low self-esteem that she sometimes felt. She hid them from even herself. Whenever they popped up, Lola took a deep breath and swallowed them back down without the benefit of a "chaser."

When she got the diagnosis from her doctor that she had yet another STD, Lola went on autopilot and visited the great river of denial. Later that night when Calvin showed up wanting their usual romp, Lola didn't want to send him away unsatisfied. Fearing an argument with him, she submitted to sex.

No, she thought, *some things I will take to the grave.*

The bitter lesson of "hear no evil speak no truth" was seared into Lola's consciousness long ago by Calvin. After confirmation that she had indeed contracted Gonorrhea, Lola tried to have an informative conversation with Calvin, who quickly flipped the script and threw accusations at her.

"Hey, Baby," she started timidly.

"What's up?" Calvin asked, never missing a beat as he smothered her body lavishly with kisses.

"I've been having pains and issues in my lower abdomen," ...

"Girl, you better not be telling me what I think you are trying to say," he interrupted looking up at her with both threatening and accusatory eyes. "What?" he demanded.

Calvin pushed Lola away from him and held her at arm's length as he perused her body and inspected her lower stomach.

"Don't play with me!" he said sternly.

"Nothing!" Lola laughed out loud. Lola's mouth suddenly became dry, and a glass of wine was all that she wanted. As she pressed the bowl of the long-stemmed wine glass to the side of her now perspiring face, Lola knew that she had to turn this train wreck around.

Oh my God, I can't even remember that one guy's name, she thought to herself. But deep in her heart, Lola knew that it was Calvin. She knew that he was the carrier and that his wife had already been privy to the information. *Maybe that's why Vicky kept kicking him out.* Her mind was a melting pot of images and scenarios that she could not control, so she downed her wine and poured another glass.

"Good 'cause I was about to drag you down to Planned Parenthood myself!" Calvin interrupted. "Ain't nobody got time for all of that! This is not that kind of Party!"

"Well, you don't have anything to worry about in that regards," Lola quickly added, trying not to ruffle Calvin's feathers any further.

Lola's only resolve at that point was to get as drunk as humanly possible and to lie down with Calvin. Slowly pouring her third glass of wine, she looked at Calvin lying on the bed and felt a pang of sadness. This was something that she knew she would have to bear alone. If Calvin weren't the one that gave her the STD then she would place the blame on Mike or "what's his name." Her head spun feverishly over the thought of all parties involved, and she climbed on top of Calvin as a warrior princess incarnate!

"I'm not trying to hear all of that," Calvin finished saying.

"No, don't worry about it," Lola said softly. "I'm okay. Now, shhh," she said, comforting him with each thrust of her now aching body. "Relax baby," Lola repeatedly whispered to him, as she rocked him into submission with the rhythm of her body.

Chapter Six:
"Ghetto" is a State of Mind

Cindy sat robotically stirring her drink at the bar. The smell of stale cigarettes engulfed the entirety of the dimly lit room. Looking up at the clock, she shook her head at the nerve of her daughter. Her selfishness, her mother thought, was evident in the fact that it was a full half hour past their appointed meeting time and Lola had not yet arrived.

"I'm not putting up with your whoring around, girl!" Cindy screamed at Lola. "I don't know who you think you are! If you had kept your legs closed in the first place you would not be in this predicament! How many times have I told you to be careful? All those little boys sniffing around you want from you is some booty! And here you are, "Miss Stupid", lying down with who knows who and now you're sticking out pregnant!" Lola's mother continued to holler at her. "And if you think you're keeping that baby, and playing house up in here, you've got another thing coming! Not in here! I'm the only mama in my house! Your daddy and I have enough problems paying the bills without another mouth to feed."

Cindy slammed the door to Lola's bedroom behind her and left Lola alone on the bed crying. Suddenly the door burst back open, and Cindy continued with her rant. "I'm making a call to Planned Parenthood in the morning, and we're going down there! I don't want to hear anything else about it with your trifling behind!"

her mother said sharply, and again left Lola's room slamming the door behind her.

But that day never came for Lola. Later that night Lola climbed out of her bedroom window and into the arms of Willie. He had been given an update as to Cindy's plans for the following day and waited outside of her window to take Lola home with him. That was the last time that Lola and her mother had spoken.

Lola was 17 years old when she left home. Even at the pleading of her father and sister she never returned. There was no time for her to finish high school, or even the hope of continued education with a brand-new baby to take care of. Willie's parents did as much for her as they could, but Lola could not help but feel uncomfortable in their home after overhearing his mother tell Willie's father that their son had been "trapped by that girl!"

On Lola's 18th birthday, she and Willie got married. Carrying their young child in her arms and with her heart racing a mile a minute they said their "I do's" at the courthouse in the judge's private chambers. Their only witnesses that day were the court's bailiff and an unnamed clerk. The young couple took up residence on the seeder side of town where Willie spent his days working on cars to make a living for them.

Lola settled into her surroundings and embraced the lifestyle of the streets. The fast paced, hustle and bustle of the neighborhood with its corner drug dealers and streetwalkers were fascinating to her. It was worlds away from where she grew up or how her parents raised her. When Lola walked down the street with Little Willie, the whistles and jeers from the men when she walked by made her feel attractive and desirable. And feeling attractive was a feeling that was a far cry from her experience in high school. Lola's blotchy skin and pimple covered face was the source of her constantly being teased.

The men on the block didn't seem to notice those things. So, when Lola walked by a group of men loitering on the street, she made sure to put a little extra switch in her hips and to hold her chest out in confidence. That confidence is what got her the attention of Marvin. He was an older man with a fancy car and the promises of a shopping spree and money to get her hair done.

Lola was secretly impressed with Marvin's world. The folks in the neighborhood called him "Big Man". He presented Lola as his lady and his friends rolled out the red carpet for her when she was with him. There were visits to the mall, shopping sprees and extra cash in her purse. When her husband, Willie confronted her one day after seeing her out in the neighborhood with "Big Man," Lola was shocked.

She had left Little Willie alone in his crib, and Willie was enraged at her thoughtlessness. Lola vehemently denied the existence of their relationship until finally, in a rage of insults thrown towards Willie, Lola let him know that he was not her "Daddy" and that she was her own person who deserved a better life. A life that no longer included him. On that sour note, Lola packed her and Little Willie's things and left.

When Lola arrived on the doorstep of Big Man's flat, she quickly learned her first lesson on expendability. Marvin's wife opened the door and told her that her husband could be found at Sukie's corner bar with his "other" woman! Looking the woman up and down with her over-sized housecoat on and her dirty house shoes that made a slapping noise as she slid across the floor, made Lola indignant.

"She needs to lose some weight!" she thought to herself as she rotated Willie Jr. from one hip to the other and headed back down the front steps. Marvin gave her a few dollars for a couple of nights stay in a run-down motel in the downtown area and sent her on her way. Determined not to cry or go running back to her mother's house, Lola accepted her lot.

She would take the advice that her mother as well as her cousin, Gina had been throwing her way for years and she used what she had to get what she needed. That was the making of her independence. Life had taught Lola how to finagle and slip her way through the cracks of life. She learned how to use her assets to get what she wanted, and she was never too long without a job. Whether it was slinging fast food or wiping "butts" in the old folk's home she was determined to survive. And she did.

The dark, dank atmosphere of the "Blinking Cat Bar" slapped Lola in the face as she entered the room. She quickly snatched off her sunglasses and searched the room for Cindy. There in the back corner of the bar, she saw her mother. She stood waving her arms signaling Lola over to the small table. It was evident to Lola that Cindy had been running a tab and that she was close to being intoxicated. Lola could remember a time when seeing a drink placed anywhere in the vicinity of Cindy would have caused her anger, but not today. Somehow Lola did not care.

Today, she just felt tired. She was tired of all the antics and bull crap! Lola sat down across from her mother and slowly and calmly crossed her legs. She looked at her mother up and down and let out a little sigh.

"Look," Lola began speaking to Cindy. "I'm not going to be here long; I just wanted to meet with you to see how you are doing and to tell you, "Thank you." Lola spoke slowly and deliberately to her mother and then paused to pull a pack of cigarettes from her coat pocket and lit one up.

She inhaled deeply waiting for her mother to respond, but Cindy sat in silence.

"Thank you?" Cindy finally repeated questioning Lola.

"Yeah," Lola continued. "Jewel and Daddy told me about how you were there for me while I was in the hospital but..."

"Thank you?" Cindy repeated, cutting her daughter off. "Baby girl, you just don't get it, do you?" she said reaching across the table for Lola's cigarette that she had laid down in the ashtray and took a long pull from it.

"Enlighten me then, Cindy," Lola said trying to restrain herself and keep calm.

"All your life you've been nothing but trouble." Cindy began. "I thought if I did for you and brought you up in style and comfort that you could make something out of yourself," she said with disdain towards Lola. "Now, you're just another ghetto cliché, working a minimum wage job, collecting your food stamps each month like the rest of those 'hood rats' you hang with!" Cindy snapped at her daughter.

"Oh my God!" Lola interjected, irritated by the direction of the conversation.

"Okay, Cindy," she conceded to her mother throwing her hands up and pushing herself back from the table in an attempt to leave.

"That's Mama to you, and don't you forget it!" Cindy shouted at Lola in a firm tone.

"Oh, so now it's Mama, huh?" Lola snapped back angrily. "Now you want me to call you, Mama? What happened to the big ol' bad, Cindy? Big ol' bad, drunk, cheating on your husband, slapping your children down the steps, Cindy!? Huh, Mama? Huh?" Lola repeated in anger and frustration at how the afternoon had taken such an ugly turn. "I'm done!" she snapped at her mother and snatched up her purse and coat and marched out of the bar.

Lola sat in the parking lot of the bar in anger and tears. She had let Cindy get the best of her; she felt that she had shown her weakness to Cindy and that Cindy had pounced on it. How could a mother and daughter be so far apart? How could words get so tangled up and take off on a path of their own?

Part of Lola wanted to run back into the bar and tell her mother that she loved her needed her and was sorry, but she just could not. Something in her felt broken. Something within Lola seemed to be blocked and forever closed off, and she had neither the strength nor inclination to fix it. She was indeed tired.

Of all the things that Cindy could say to Lola, this seemed to be the cruelest.

"How could she be so heartless?" Lola asked herself, allowing her memories to pull her back to the time in her life when she needed her mother the most, but Cindy abandoned her.

Lola thought it was all a joke when Lanny Chester asked to see what color panties she was wearing after their eighth-grade English class. He was so good looking to Lola, and someone who she thought would never pay her any attention. As Lola and Abby sat in English class talking that day, a paper airplane hit Lola on the top of her head, and she turned around to see Lanny Chester smiling at her. The two girls giggled, and Lola put on her sweetest smile. The eighth-grade basketball team was playing in their spring tournament that night, and Lanny was their star player. He sat in the back of the class with his tall, lanky body draped over his desk and his legs resting on the seat in front of him.

"I think somebody likes you," Rita said in a "sing-song" mocking voice to Lola.

"He has a girlfriend, or did you forget?" Lola replied.

"Yeah, but I heard he quit her," said Rita.
Self-consciously Lola began to twitch in her seat at the thought of Lanny starring at her. It was an uncomfortable yet exciting feeling to be the object of his attention.

"Hey, I'm having a birthday party this weekend. You wanna come?" Lanny asked, before lunch as Lola stopped by her locker.

"Yeah," she responded and continued to pick at the combination lock on her locker.

"But you have to be my girlfriend first," Lanny joked to

Lola.

Before Lola could reply to him, Lanny planted a quick kiss on her cheek, and he took off for his next class.

"He did what!?" Rita screamed, wanting to hear all the details.

"Yeah, he asked me to be his girlfriend and kissed me goodbye!" Lola exclaimed to her impatient friend.

"I hate you!" declared Rita jokingly and made her way down the hall to her next class.

All throughout the day, Lanny made it his business to randomly pop his head into each class that Lola was attending to blow her a kiss and to give her a little wink. Lola found herself delighted at the thought of having such a high profile "basketball star" as a potential boyfriend and spent the rest of the school day on cloud nine.

"May I walk you home?" Lanny asked Lola as she walked to her last class of the day.

"Oh, okay," she replied, and gave him a big smile.

"What color panties you got on?" he whispered into her ear and took off running down the hall.

Lanny turned his tall, lean body around as he now ran backward and jogged in place waiting for her reply. Suddenly, without restraint Lola yelled after him "Pink!" then blushed at her audacity.

During their walk home Lola felt happy and special while Lanny held her hand and told her how pretty she was.

"So why don't you have a boyfriend with your pretty self?" Lanny teased Lola as they walked away from the school and crossed over the football field.

"Cause my mama said I had to keep my nose in my books and stay out of trouble," she replied with a shyness that she wasn't quite comfortable with. "Plus," she continued, "I think you say that to all of the girls."

"Just the fine ones like you," he stated, and they continued to walk.

The direction of their walk had taken on an unfamiliar look to Lola because her house was entirely in the other direction.

"Why are we walking so far out of the way?" she asked Lanny when she could no longer identify her surroundings.

"Because I want to show you something special," he replied grabbing her hand and squeezing it tighter.

When Lanny told Lola that he wanted to show her the special place where he went to be alone and to think she followed him through the park and along the railroad tracks. She was exuberant over the fact that he would share such an intimate part of his life with her. It was something that made Lola feel warm and significant.

With Jewel now gone off to college and with Cindy working so much, Lola had begun to feel a bit isolated and alone at home. The times when her father actually came home had grown fewer and scarcer since he and Cindy fought so frequently. Lola secretly longed for someone to laugh and talk with. The possibility of her now having a boyfriend in Lanny was the best feeling in the world.

When Lola and Lanny entered the old, abandoned factory on Melon Street, her heart began to beat faster, and she couldn't catch her breath at that moment. There was something eerie about the darkness of the building during the middle of the day that shook her to the core, and she felt fear. The dampness of the building with its broken windows reminded Lola of a haunted house and it made her afraid.

"Now, little Lola, let me see those pink panties that you teased me about earlier."

"What?" Lola questioned. "I was just playing..."

But before Lola could finish her sentence, Lanny had covered her mouth with the fullness of his lips, and she closed her eyes. Lola chalked it up to the fact that Lanny's last class of the day was PE, and that he had taken a shower before he left the school. Lola recognized the cologne from her daddy's bathroom shelf. Sometimes when her father was away on long over the road drives Lola would go into his medicine cabinet and open a bottle of his cologne. It made her feel closer to her father and to not miss him so much.

When Lola breathed in the intoxicating smells of Lanny, any uneasy thoughts that she may have had were put to rest. On this day when Lanny swooped Lola closer to him, her body betrayed her, and she gave in to his firm arm around her waist. Lola closed her eyes like she saw the women in the movies do and breathed in the gloriousness of his scent. She became so enraptured by the feelings of his wet kisses that she hardly noticed that Lannie had pulled her to the dirty ground and was removing her underwear.

"Wait a minute!" Lola shouted, coming back to reality.

"You know you like it," Lanny stated coyly and began to forcefully pen her body down.

Suddenly out of the shadows Lola could see movement from behind the crates. They were the familiar images of legs running towards them, but she could not quite make them out. While she lay pent under Lanny, her suspicions were confirmed by the clear sight of Lanny's older brothers, Melvin and Charles Chester.

"Lola get your fast tail in this house!" Cindy shouted through her bedroom window as a few of the neighborhood boys stopped to talk to her one afternoon.

"Girl, you are looking kind of fly," the older one said to Lola as she stood talking to her friend Rita in front of her house.

"Yeah, I bet you can't pull that!" his brother Charles joked with him.

The two boys lived in the neighborhood with their parents and a younger brother who was a classmate of Lola's. The older boys were constantly getting into trouble in the neighborhood and Lola could not stand them. At night, they would run up and down the alley behind the house which Lola lived in and tip over the garbage cans or spray-paint the garage doors of residents in the area. Everyone knew who they were but because their parents were "big shots" around town they seemed to get away with everything.

"Y'all need to get from in front of my mama's house talking all of that smack!" Lola shouted back at the boys in the sassiest voice that she could muster. "Cause ain't nobody gonna 'pull' me! You might as well get from around here!" she continued sassing them and rolled her eyes at the boys. "Take a picture it'll last longer!" she screamed in their direction when she found them yet staring at her from a distance.

Lying on the cold, dirty floor with her pretty, pink panties tossed to the side of her head, Lola felt that she had asked for it. Why didn't she just ignore Lanny when he asked her about her panties? Why didn't she tell Rita to wait for her after school? Lola fought and screamed for them to stop, but they held her down forcefully. Melvin stuffed an old rag in her mouth and cursed at her profusely as he reminded her of the day that she mouthed off at them while in front of her house.

First, it was Lanny, then Melvin, then Charles, then Lanny again… each one was taking their turn deflowering Lola. When all the fight had gone from Lola, she found it easier to just lie still and concentrate on her breathing and that spider crawling on the broken window above her head. If she could just breath through it maybe it wouldn't hurt so much, she thought. The pulling of her thigh bones made her feel as if she was going to be ripped in half.

Is that a rat, she thought as she lay there; the back of her head scraping the dirty concrete floor with each thrust. *Of course, that's a rat you stupid girl!* She continued with the dialogue in her head. *You are in a vacant building getting raped by three boys because you were stupid enough to think that one of them liked you!* Lola rhythmically and methodically drowned out their laughter and grunts with her own thoughts. *You are so stupid, you are so stupid, you are so stupid, you are so stupid, you are so stupid.* Her words, like their thrusts, went on for what seemed like hours. *You are so stupid.*

Lola stood on the back screened-in porch, her body in shock; she could barely hold herself up. The blood trickled down the young girl's legs spotting her white socks. Lola could not get the words to come out of her mouth. She stood frozen.

Cindy was in the kitchen fixing her lunch for that evening when she thought she saw something on the back porch. She turned around and studied the figure slowly before she realized that it was Lola. Cindy slowly wiped her hands on her apron, and without taking her eyes off the child, she walked gingerly towards her as if she was seeing a ghost.

"What have you done?!" she screamed at Lola.

"It wasn't my fault," Lola stammered. "I told him I was just playing!" Lola screamed hysterically finally able to let go of her emotions. "It wasn't' my fault!" She repeated collapsing in her mother's arms.

"You have ruined yourself, girl, you have just ruined yourself!"

Those were the only words that Lola's mother could offer her. Lola was barely 14, when her world changed forever. The trajectory of which no one could imagine. A warm bath and a lecture were Lola's medicine. There were no trips to the emergency room, no impromptu visits to the family doctor for fear of gossip, and Cindy kept Lola away from school for the rest of the semester. She informed the principal that Lola had come down with a case of Mononucleosis. For the rest of the month, Cindy kept her eyes on Lola's frame, her diet, and her menstrual cycle to ward off any pregnancy scares.

By early summer Lola was sent to spend time with her grandmother, Pearl and her cousin, Gina in the country. Nanna Pearl taught Lola about Jesus, how to make cornbread and how to play solitaire, while Gina taught Lola how to never be a victim again.

Lola sat on the raggedy dock overlooking Rowels Bay and threw rocks into the water. She wanted to hate everything about the country, but she couldn't. The flies, mosquitoes, and loud, nightly chirping were enough to drive her insane. But there was something about the sweet smell of the hot earth after the rain that Lola liked. The all-consuming thickness of the fallen dew on the blades of grass made her feel such melancholy.

"Hey," Gina said while coming up behind Lola and squatting beside her.

"Hey," Lola said squinting and holding her hand horizontally across her eyes to protect her from the bright glare as she spoke.

"Thought you'd' be out here. Granny said you bout to be as skinny and sickly as that there piglet in the barn if you don't get you sumtin' to eat!" Gina advised her cousin with her heavy, southern accent. "You know what you done wrong, don't ya?"

Gina's accent was so thick that at times Lola could hardly understand her.

"What? What I done wrong?" Lola repeated purposely trying to match her cousin's broken English.

"Well, for starters, you shudda just rode them boys back, but you fought, didn't you?" the young girl asked never waiting for Lola's response. "Yep, see, that right dere, dat's where you went all da way wrong! Chile, gals down here in these parts get runa train alls the time. Shoot, if you ain't been run up, then keep living. Granny says they been running trains since she was a girl."

"What do you mean "running a train?" Lola asked Gina.

"That's what they call it down here; that what's done gone and happened to you!" she stated in a matter-of-fact tone and continued to throw rocks into the bay.

Lola didn't want to discuss the matter any further; however, Gina was 2 years older than Lola, and she seemed to possess a wealth of information that a 14-year-old might need, so she kept quiet.

"What do you mean I shudda rode the boys back?" Lola asked Gina, still trying to understand what her cousin was referring to.

"See," Gina explained, "there's a thin line between victim and victor. If you gone lose, wouldn't it be better to lose by your own rules?" she asked. "The way it was told to me was you gone lose any way you put it. But that loss you had was a bad loss!"

Gina never took her eyes off the water as she spoke to Lola and continued to throw rocks into the bay as though she was hypnotized.

"The way them boys tore through you, done left you in a world of hurt and pain."

Lola looked at her cousin and used all the restraint within her to keep herself from pushing Gina into the water.

"You was robbed sure enough, but you coulda turned the page on 'em and let the diva in you out and gave dem boys a run for they money."

Slowly, like an overly concerned parent, Gina turned to Lola, and in a calm controlled voice, she said, "Haven't you heard? There's power in the Punani!"

Lola had never heard that word before, and the look on her face was evident to Gina.

"Stick with me, I'll help 'ya out! I see now all that city living ain't done nothing but caused you to get fat!" She laughed.

Lola and Gina sat for hours on the dock that day where Gina taught Lola about the power of the "Punani."

When Lola returned home from her summer in the country with Nanna Pearl and Cousin Gina, she was a different Lola. The once young girl that had left the city broken and ashamed was now a more matured, outspoken, and self-assured young woman. Lola's walk, talk, and demeanor now embodied that of confidence and attitude. The small things which bothered Lola before didn't bother her anymore. Lola had cultivated in that short time a harder exterior and a "centeredness" that harbored between haughty and arrogance.

"When you get back to the city, don't go fo'gettin 'bout yo cousin now," Gina warned Lola, as she braided Lola's hair on the front porch the night before Lola was scheduled to leave.

Lola fought back her tears and told Gina that they would be sisters forever. Lola had never had the kind of bond with anyone like she had formed with Gina.

She didn't have to pretend with Gina, and her cousin was able to pierce through Lola's bubble by using her silly country sayings and southern drawl and get to Lola's heart.

At times, it felt to Lola as though Gina was being mean and contrary, but Gina always built Lola back up with her encouraging words and affirmations. Gina came to know all of Lola's weaknesses. She taught Lola how to turn the negatives that she was feeling into ammunition.

On the train ride back home, Lola reminisced over her summer and laughed to herself as she remembered Nanna Pearl throwing her shoe at the girls when she found them smoking cigarettes in the back of her old pickup truck. And how she had almost drowned in the creek when one of Gina's boyfriends told her to jump from the cliff; and that he would catch her.

But most of all Lola cherished those long, detailed "inappropriate" sex talks. Their whispering under the sheets as she listened to the intricate details of Gina's sexual escapades with Jarvis. Those were the stories that Lola loved the most. Those were the stories that she wanted to emulate in her own life.

"Didn't his tongue feel all wet and nasty?" Lola interrupted her cousin as Gina tried to explain the joys of oral sex to Lola.

"Just because you done had some rough and tumble type sex don't mean that's how it's 'spose to be," she replied to Lola and leapt to her feet and ran to her closet.

Gina began to giggle as she pushed her clothing to the

far side of the rack and revealed to Lola her secret stash of dirty magazines.

"Girl, how did you get to be so nasty?" Lola laughed aloud, as she continued to examine each page.

The images of naked female bodies spread out between the pages of the magazines caught Lola off guard. But something began to happen to her perception of them when she saw the lust and desire on the men's faces. As the images began to repeat themselves, Lola saw the power of the "Punani," and she wanted it.

"Now all you need is a willing victim," Gina laughed.

Never in her life did Lola think she would undertake such an education in the middle of the country under the watchful eye of her saintly grandmother and her wayward cousin. From that day forward Lola vowed to be in control of her sexuality, and since it seemed to her that it could be used against her, she decided that it was going to be her weapon to use as she pleased and to protect herself when she felt threatened.

Lola never saw the Chester Boys again. When she returned from Grandma Pearl's things were a lot different at home. Jewel said it was because of Cindy. She greeted her little sister with open arms and in tears. Lola's ordeal was something that Jewel naturally did not want to talk about. She was happy to have Lola back home safe and sound, and Jewel was glad that Lola seemed to have a new attitude.

After Cindy put Lola on the train to her grandmother's house, she began her reign of terror against the Chester family. Hysterically, Jewel laughed as she began to tell her little sister of the night that Cindy went to the Chester's home drunk and broke out all the windows, screaming, "the Chester boys were a bunch of rapists," and threatening to set fire to their home.

Shortly after, the Chester's quietly moved away from the neighborhood. It was hard to believe that Cindy would do anything in a protective mode for her, Lola thought, but she accepted it as truth and tried to move on with her life. The Chester boys and the events on Melon Street were never spoken of again.

Chapter Seven:
The Death of a Dream

She lay in a heap on the ground in the pouring rain. Nothing in her life had prepared her for this moment. What had she done in all her young life to deserve such a thing? She called out to God to have mercy on her and to ease this pain, but heaven it seemed, had closed its doors on Lola.

The smell of the flowers in the room was thick with a deep aroma of sorrow. The penetrating organ music made Lola want to throw up. The guests were packed in like sardines as they tried to find an available place to sit. Jewel and Tiffany each held Lola up by the arms as they walked around for the viewing. The look on Vicky's face, the sheer tragic, pain of it all shocked Lola as she respectfully paused to glance over at the row set aside for family. She had no right she conceded, to disturb their grief.

As Lola came closer to the casket her knees gave way, and the two women on her side quickly tightened their grip around her, and she composed herself. Calvin looked so old lying there, his body which at one point in time for Lola seemed to be the epitome of a Greek god, now lay motionless and small. The dark, grey suit which he wore seemed to add years to his actual age. All the words unspoken, and things left unsaid between the two lovers were now lost to Lola forever.

As she left the viewing of Calvin's body, her eyes fell upon Miss Ruby, Calvin's mother. She sat slumped over in the arms of a male, sobbing softly into her handkerchief. Lola wanted to run over to her and fling herself upon the elderly woman's lap and hold her tightly. She wanted to tell Miss Ruby that she knew exactly how it felt to lose Calvin; Lola wanted to tell her that she loved her son and that the times that they were together were the best of her life. Lola wanted somebody, anybody in that row to know that Calvin was her life. Instead, she held her chest tightly fearing that it would explode at that moment and moved stealthily by as Jewel held her up firmly.

"My mama doesn't play!" Calvin told Lola as they lay together one night. "Naw, Miss. Ruby do not play!" he reiterated. "She is a sure enough, fire and brimstone woman of God," he said laughing.

Lola relished the thought of meeting Calvin's mother and would sit and listen to the stories about her many antics, imagining that she knew her, and that Miss Ruby was a part of her life. She longed for Calvin to present her to his mother as the one whom he loved. In Lola's mind, her day was coming. If Calvin and Vicky continued their road of marital discourse and discontentment, she was sure that she would be the next Mrs. Clampten.

Thoughts of dignified luncheons, where the two ladies sat and ate crumpets and drank tea was Lola's secret fantasy. She wanted and needed that acceptance. The rose-colored glasses that she viewed life from was the result of too many "lifetime TV movies" and imaginings. The reality of the matter was that Miss Ruby and Lola were worlds apart. The fast-paced, rambunctious life which Lola enjoyed would not sit well with Miss Ruby.

The Death of a Dream

She had told her son many times before that the reason for his problems and malcontent was because of his disobedience to God and the lack of His presence in Calvin's life. Stating, with a finger, pointed towards him in warning that "the wages of sin, is death!" as she put it. Calvin would never disrupt his mother's sanctity with the insult of Lola.

"You know, we really don't have to go to the grave site," Tiffany said to Lola as they walked through the parking lot of the church to get into Jewel's car.

"I know," Lola said dryly. "But I want to be there," ...she trailed off.

Tiffany looked at Lola's sister, Jewel and the two of them nodded in agreement of supporting Lola in her decision.

"That should have been me putting him to rest and not her!" Lola whimpered. "I didn't even get a say in anything!" she cried letting her true feelings pour out. "Calvin loved me not her! She sobbed. "I didn't even get a chance to give remarks, nothing!" She cried uncontrollably. "I couldn't even ..."

"Shhh," Jewel said in a soothing voice rubbing her sister's back. "As long as Calvin knew."

"But he's gone!" She shouted back at her sister.

The two women consoled Lola as best as they could, and Lola sat in silence for the rest of the drive.

"What in the world are you wearing, girl?" Calvin said as he opened the front door.

Lola had greeted him partially naked with a big, red bow tied around her waist.
"Happy birthday, baby!" she exclaimed, as she turned around so that he could view all her nakedness.

"Dang!" Calvin stated and began to tear the ribbon from Lola's waist.
"How long can you stay?" Lola asked Calvin as she unbuttoned his pants and went down on her knees.

"I only have about a half hour, because Vicky made dinner arrangements with my parents."

Lola felt as though she had been slapped in the face.

"Really? She said looking up at him from the carpeted floor.

"Shh!" he commented. "Do your thang, Baby Girl" he directed her, and Lola continued pleasuring him.

Calvin zipped up his pants hastily after his climax and patted Lola on the head.
"Sorry, but I gotta go," he said with a smile.

Lola exhaled with a sigh and tried to locate her robe. A feeling of embarrassment came over her as she found herself scrabbling upon her knees in search of a cover-up. The headlights from a car turning into its parking spot outside of her bedroom window illuminated her nakedness. And for the first time in all her dealings with Calvin, Lola felt ashamed and vulnerable.

She had endured for the sake of being with Calvin the

day after Valentine's Day, the day before Thanksgiving, eating Chinese food from a plastic carry-out bag alone on her birthday, and she even put up with celebrating Christmas on the day after; all for the sake of being with him. But somehow, picking herself up off her bedroom floor after having performed fellatio on this man and having him pat her on the head like a dog ignited a fury within her.

"Do your thang, baby girl?" She questioned Calvin as he fastened his watch upon his wrist and collected his spare change from the top of the nightstand. "That's all I get? You run in here for a quick 'service,' which I oblige like a 'pro' and all I get from you is, 'do your thang?' Precisely what is my 'thang' Calvin? You do realize that you just patted me on the head like a dog while I sucked you off, right? You do realize, that don't you?" Lola said, her anger bubbling over.

"I don't have time for this tonight, Lo," Calvin responded, unmoved by her theatrics. "Why are you doing this now?" he asked.

Lola took a deep breath and searched for the correct phrasing before she spoke. She didn't want to say anything that she would regret later, but she needed to blow off a little steam. Through all that she had endured, Lola had finally come to the point where she wanted to demand more. She was tired of taking the back seat.

"You like the simplicity of how we get down, don't you baby?" Calvin whispered into her ear as he stuffed his pockets with his keys and simultaneously checked his appearance in the mirror. "You like that thing I do when I do that thing that I do to you... don't you?" he teased her and simulated a sexy little gyration.

"Don't 'handle' me, Calvin," Lola said as she resentfully tried to free herself from his hug. She felt like a spoiled child facing an incumbent tantrum.

"Give me some shuga," he whispered in her ear seductively trying to placate her by firmly pressing his lips against hers for one of his "Calvin-makes-everything-better" kisses.

Lola swooned as she pulled away from him. She steadied herself and tried to remain upbeat, while hiding this obvious "hit" to her ego.

"I'm gonna call you tomorrow, okay?" he stated, and closed the door behind him.

That was the last time that Lola saw Calvin alive.

"Way to speak up for yourself!" Lola pouted, and watched through the blinds in her bedroom window as Calvin got in his car and pulled off.

In all areas of her life, Lola was a warrior. She stood firm on most of the decisions that she made regarding how she lived her life. She spoke up for herself when she felt undue pressure from her family and questioned authority at work. But when it came to her love life, Lola was a wreck.

"It can't just be the sex," Tiffany scolded her friend when Lola spoke of the night's events at breakfast the next morning.

"I just didn't want to make waves," Lola said sheepishly.

"What are you really afraid of, Lo?" Tiffany questioned.

"I'm in love, Tiff, don't you get it. I'm trying to protect what I have…"

"You might be in love but what is Calvin in? I'll tell you what he's in…" Tiffany continued, picking up momentum in her direct approach with her friend. "He's in lust! That's about all! I know that you don't want to hear this, but I'm your friend, and I hate this look on you, girl! What's your end game, Lo?" She demanded to know. "What is your end game? Have you thought about that? Have you? I didn't think so! You have put your whole life on hold for him and for what? What are you getting from this 'relationship' that you're in?" Tiffany demanded to know stopping to insert her imaginary quotation marks around the word relationship. "…So that he can run up in here and get his jollies and leave you the same way that he found you…waiting!"

Lola's "street game" was fierce. She took a back seat to few when it came to trash talking, flirting, or making her intentions known to the object of her desire, for the men as well as the women. Lola talked just as loud and slick as any man could. However, she had met her match in Calvin. Where Calvin was concerned, Lola had no voice. She had surrendered her soul over to him, and it was silently killing her.

"I can't believe you let him play you like that Lo!" Tiffany said interrupting Lola's train of thought. "Look, I gotta go," she said, trying her best not to grab Lola and to shake some sense into her. "I'll call you later, kiss the kids for me," she said and proceeded to pick up her bag and leave.

"I love you too!" Lola said sarcastically, as her friend left the restaurant.

Lola wanted a cigarette! It was too early in the morning to be trying to explain and defend her relationship with Calvin to Keisha. She sipped the remainder of her coffee and slowly surveyed the coffee shop. It was Saturday morning, and the kids had spent the night with their grandfather so, Lola had the entire day to herself. She didn't feel her usual jovial self after her conversation with Tiffany. It was supposed to be her planned day of pampering, which was to include a movie and a pedicure, but Lola had lost her desire for it. The weight of all her burdens weighed so heavy upon her that she was feeling stuck.

Lola waved to her waitress to bring her another cup of coffee, and when it arrived, she played with the spoon, making continuous stirs in her drink as she contemplated her lot.

"I need a plan B," she laughed suddenly to herself. "I need a good old-fashioned plan B or maybe an all-inclusive Hawaiian getaway," she mused, "complete with a good old fashioned 'cabana boy'."

Lola allowed the fantasy of her imagined Hawaiian Vacation to lull her mood into an upward lift. She imagined herself in a beautiful beach chair, with her feet in the sand basking away. It was these kinds of scenarios that enabled Lola to get through her trying times. Her imagination floated her away and the very thing which was bothering her melted under the sun of her concoctions.

Lola had promised herself a trip to paradise since the birth of Trina. The funds that Nick contributed to his daughter allowed her a little luxury that she kept secret from those closest to her. Not even Tiffany was privy to the knowledge of who Trina's father was. When Jewel would remind Lola of her "lifestyle", many times she had to refrain from snapping back at her in anger and letting her know that with the help of your fantastic job, "we" are doing just fine! But Lola never took her bait. That had been one of the only areas in her life where she was able to show some restraint.

"May I join you?" a familiar voice interrupted Lola's musing.

Lola looked up from her coffee and recognized the familiar face of an old lover, Scotty Bonds. Without waiting for an answer, Scotty slipped into the booth across from Lola. She couldn't help but smile in delight as he picked up the check that the waitress had laid upon the table and asked to buy her a refill. She smiled to herself and thought about her favorite saying which she repeated in jest to Tiffany regularly, "There's no better way to get over an old guy than to get under a new one." However, Scotty was not new he was someone from Lola's past that she had become bored with and dismissed. Lola coyly smiled in direct answer to his offer and exhaled as she studied Scotty.

This day just might not be a total bust after all, she thought.

"How have you been?" he inquired.

"I'm much better now!" Lola replied as she allowed her mind to instantaneously take her back to the last time that they were together.

Lola had promised herself that she would exercise more self-restraint after her recent medical set back a few months earlier; she had kept her promise pretty well. She hadn't brought any new men into her bed, but the thought of being with Scotty felt like an exception to this rule because, she told herself, Scotty was an old contender.

"Hold on to your panties," she scolded herself when she felt those familiar urges surface.

Instead of going into her usual "pounce" mode, Lola decided to enjoy the pace and the chase. She slowly began to make love to his mouth as he talked to her. Each word that fell from his lips Lola played with. Every gesture that he performed she slowed them down in her brain into slow motion.

"You're a predator," Eric told her one night as they finished their romp in the back hallway of Lola's favorite night club. "You raped me!" he joked, as he zipped up his pants and smiled broadly wiping the sweat from his brow.

"It doesn't take a girl long to see what she wants and to grab it," she proudly stated and left him standing in the hall as she retreated into the Ladies' room.
"But those days are over," she thought bringing her imaginings back to the diner and the beautiful specimen in front of her.

"Why don't we get out of here?" Scotty asked Lola. "We could go to my place and get reacquainted," he continued as Lola sat across from him smiling.

"Ooo," Lola moaned in her most provocative voice.
"...And what, pray tell, would we do after that?" she goaded him encouraging him to continue with his proposition.

Scotty went into great detail of how they would spend

the afternoon, and the things that he would do to her body. Lola smiled seductively as he spoke and enjoyed the fantasy.

Lola was a naughty girl. It was a simple fact. She had given up on her years of self-analysis and the contemplations of her ways, and she simply accepted who she was. Her fantasies about taking Scotty home with her were overwhelming. She knew that he could make her feel 'right' again. *Yep, a few good strokes from him would balance me out*, she laughed to herself. He would be her delicious distraction. *Like a moth to a flame*, Lola thought as reached across the table slowly and took his hands. *I have teased this fool long enough.*

"Why don't you call me next week, Baby," she said abruptly, pouring water on her incendiary thoughts.

Lola knew for certain that she had thrown water on his flame. Yes, Lola was feeling fine. Her little pep talk with Scotty was the medicine that she needed to carry on. When she arrived home, she put on her favorite music and her sweatpants and began to spring clean. The mounting dirty clothes that she had left unattended for weeks were starting to smell up the apartment, so she went into housekeeping mode and began the task.

Lola never allowed her mind to wander back on her last meeting with Calvin. She knew he would call her soon. Enough time had passed between them for her to get over any negative feelings that she may have been harboring against him. After all, she thought, Calvin was her love. She would always love him, and she would always forgive his slights.

The "call" came the next night from Tiffany.

"Girl, are you alright?" Her friend asked her with concern.

"Yeah, it's just a little storm, Tiff! I'm a big girl. I'm not afraid of the lightning," Lola laughed unaware of the freight train that was about to hit her.

"Lola," Tiffany said sternly and cautiously, "Turn on the news."

Lola flipped on the local news channel and watched a most curious scene. There was a car flipped over in a ditch, and the newscaster was saying, something else that she failed to make out. Lola's mouth dropped as she heard it.

"And the victim has been identified as prominent Janistown resident, Calvin Clampten of Clampten and James Industries" the announcer seemed to be saying.

Lola grabbed her coat and ran out into the storm. She had to get to Calvin.
"Where are my keys?" she screamed. "Where is my car?" she hysterically called out to anyone that was listening. "Calvin!" ... she screamed into the rain as she fell to the ground in utter grief. "Calvin, Calvin, Calvin" ...

When Jewel received the call that evening from Tiffany regarding Calvin's death, she had a feeling that her sister Lola was in trouble. It took a few minutes for Jewel to fully process what Tiffany was saying to her on the telephone. When she was able to understand what had happened, she quickly let her husband Nick know that she needed to go and check on Lola. When

Jewel arrived in front of Lola's apartment; she found her sister sitting in a puddle of rainwater in tears. Jewel hurried to her side and tried to get Lola to get off the ground and to go inside with her.

"Jew-Jew!" Lola screamed when she saw her sister.

"I know, Lo," Jewel said trying to comfort Lola.

"But we have to get you out of this rain and out of these clothes," her sister urged pulling Lola of the ground and onto her feet.

Jewel had never seen her sister so distraught. Lola was inconsolable. As Jewel ushered Lola back into the apartment complex and into her home, she felt helpless. Lola was the youngest child, but Jewel felt that Lola had the strength of an ox. No matter what was thrown at her little sister she seemed to be resilient. Jewel tried to use as few words as she could in soothing Lola because she simply did not know what to say. Many times, in the past Jewel, had scolded Lola about Calvin. She felt that he was a despicable person and she wanted him out of her Lola's life.

At this moment Jewel felt conflicted. Lola was going to get the release that many of her family and friends wanted for her, but the shock of Calvin's death to her psychologically was something that she never bargained for.

When Tiffany and Rita showed up on the scene, the three women did their best to console their friend. Lola's hysteria was shattering for them. Jewel rummaged through Lola's medicine cabinets frantically looking for something to calm her nerves and make this night a little more bearable for her. When she found sleeping pills, the women decided that it was best to give her a dose and put her to bed.

Lola was lost. Calvin's death and the fact that she could not see him because he was not family tore her apart.

"They could have let her see him!" Rita surmised as the women sat at the kitchen table after Lola finally fell asleep.

"And say what?" Tiffany demanded. "What would Lo say, showing up to the hospital with all of that man's family sitting there in pain? I'm his lover, and I want to kiss him goodbye before you take him off to the morgue?" Tiffany asked sarcastically, "Girl, get real!"

"I know…" Jewel said dryly. "It's a bad situation all around."

"It's a good thing that the kids aren't here to see their mother like this. Where are they?" Tiffany inquired.

"They spent the weekend with my dad, Jewel said.

The moment Jewel got the call about Calvin she wanted to call her father but feared his response. John hated Calvin, and he prayed daily for Lola to come to her senses and to end things with him. Knowing her father, like she did Jewel thought that he would say "good riddance." As horrible as it felt Jewel knew that this grief was something that Lola was going to have to go through alone because no one that truly loved Lola would grieve Calvin. In their eyes, he was to blame for all of Lola's rebellions and her lifestyle. No one accepted or understood the depth and or the true intense nature of Lola. They would always and forever pin that detail upon an outside force.

She was standing under the trees at the cemetery that day, and Lola felt overwhelmed by her feelings of loss. The mere thought of having to go through the drudgery of her life without Calvin to hold was incomprehensible.

"This is some sick joke," she wanted to believe. And as they lowered Calvin's casket into the ground, she fought back the depths of her emotions. Lola motioned to the girls, and they walked back to the car with her. It was over. All of it was over.

Lola pulled down the visor on the passenger side of the car to look at herself in the mirror. Lola thought she looked as though she had aged by ten years. Where had all the time gone? And what would be her new normal?

"Pull over to Sukie's" she instructed Jewel.

"It's kind of early for a drink don't' you think?" her sister answered back to Lola.

"I know but pull over anyway and let me out I'll get an Uber home. I need to be alone. Lola said methodically.

"Lo…" Jewel said aloud in protest.

"I promise you I'm fine," she reassured her sister and added a stern glare directed towards Jewel to alleviate any more of her sister's interference. "I know what I'm doing" she added.

Lola smoothed back her hair and pulled a compress from her purse and re-applied her lipstick.

"I could use a drink!" she added with a new resolve.

Lola consciously adjusted the split in her skirt walked into Sukie's Bar that afternoon, and slowly took a seat at the bar. She reared back in her chair and slowly crossed her legs letting her split come undone to the point of distraction. From a distance, she spotted a good-looking man at the table having a smoke and chatting with a female. Lola lifted her sunglasses and raised her eyebrow in his direction. She slowly licked her lips and smiled at him-he didn't stand a chance.

Epilogue:
Are You Lola?

Some women are goody two shoes; some are direct and flirty, and others are just plain naughty! Which type of woman do you think you are based on your very own personality? Take the quiz below to explore your inner "Lola" tendencies. Remember, to be truthful to yourself while answering.

►1.) Where are you more likely to meet men when they approach you?

A. I'm a homebody and I never go out.

B. In a social setting: out dancing, parties, group dates

C. Health club, physical activities such as out walking my dog, hiking

D. Online apps, social media, Internet Dating, church socials

E. A hook up from my "ex," family friend, or someone I've been watching from afar and the timing is now right for me to move on him

F. All of the above

G. None of the above

►2.) What first attracts you about a man?

A. His physique:
"The darker the berry the sweeter the juice, and a few well-placed muscles don't hurt..."

B. His earning potential:
"I'm a high-quality woman, and I need someone to help me maintain!"

C. His lifestyle/His Swag:
"Where a man lives, what he drives, his job, and the clothes he wears speaks volumes about a man!"

D. His sex appeal and perceived endowment:
"Whoever said that size doesn't matter... lied! I need a man who's good in bed and can satisfy me."

E. All of the above

F. None of the above

► 3.) What personal qualities do you look for in a man?

A. Faithfulness:
"Once a cheater always a cheater!... I need a man that's faithful."

B. Confidence:
"I love a take-charge man in business, in love, and in the bedroom!"

C. Intelligence:
"A nerdy Mr. Peabody type of man turns me on. We can sit and hypothesize all night long!"

D. Vision and Purpose:
"There's nothing worse than being with a man who doesn't know what he's doing, or where he's going... I need an aggressive alpha male!"

E. A Mama's Boy:
"I have to be in charge!.. a 'Mama's Boy' takes direction, will spoil me the way I need to be spoiled, and will always seek my approval."

F. All of the above

G. None of the above

►4.) Which of the following is most important to you in a relationship?

A. Great sex:
"If a man does not have a large penis and knows how to please me, then I can't do a thing with him!"

B. Compatibility:
"It's important to be compatible in some things. A man has to meet me halfway."

C. Adventure:
"I hate staying at home, I love the excitement of being out and about, the man in my life has to be able to keep up with me."

D. Respect:
"Respect is earned... If he hasn't earned it, then I don't give it!"

E. Honesty:
"If he cheats on me, then I will definitely cheat on him! Time is out for the weak female...Payback is the best revenge!"

F. All of the above

G. None of the above

►5.) Why would you be considered a "good catch"? Because:

A. I'm a Strong Black woman!
"I'm independent and self-assured and very resilient."

B. I'm financially secure.
"I don't need a man to take care of me, I make my own money and my own decisions!"

C. I know how to please a man!
"I'm a lady in the streets and a freak beneath the sheets... If you can dream it, then I can achieve it!"

D. I know how to get things done!
"I have a mind for business, and a strong will for achievement. My boss mentality is always on point!"

E. I believe in God and I go to church.
"I was raised in the church, I love God, and I try to live a good life."

F. All of the above

►6.) How important is marriage to you?

A. Marriage is bondage!
"The best way to stifle a woman, is to chain her to the institution of marriage!"

B. Marriage is not for everybody:
"If a woman wants to get married it's her choice, and it should be done on her terms."

C. Marriage is my childhood dream!
"I dream and breathe of my wedding day! And I know one day it will happen for me!"

D. Marriage is a beautiful thing- sometimes.
"Enter into this Union with both caution and anticipation, because 50% of all marriages end in divorce!"

E. Marriage is God ordained:
"God said it is not good for man to be alone, I'm tired of being alone!"

►7.) What baggage do you bring into your current relationships?

A. None.
"I keep my therapist on speed dial!"

B. Low self-esteem:
"I have learned never to give up on myself, even though every man in my past relationships have cheated on me."

C. Trust issues:
"I know that every man cheats, and it's hard to believe anything they say!"

D. Promiscuity:
"Because of my sexual appetites, it's hard to just be with one man, especially if I get bored."

E. Negativity:
"Turning off the voices telling me that I must be in control, not trust, and being overly aggressive is hard for me to overcome. I'm a work in progress."

*The above quiz was intended not to shame but to reveal. Did you uncover any hidden Lola tendencies or patterns? If so, can you draw a correlation between them and your current style of thinking and behavior?

Want to know whether, based on your answers, you are Lola? Be sure to read Book 7, The Psychology of Sex!